Rhydian's Quest

A Knight's Journey

By

V S Jones

Published by New Generation Publishing in 2013

Copyright © V. S. Jones 2013

Cover illustration by Sarah J Ganniclifft

A revised edition published in paperback for the first time.

www.newgeneration-publishing.com

 New Generation **Publishing**

Part One

The
Journey

Chapter One - The Squire

In the Castle's quiet stable soon to be knighted, sat a young squire, cleaning his beloved horse's saddle. A bright new embroidered caparison of crimson and yellow lay in readiness to cover the fine leather, colours to banish sadness from anyone's heart. Tomorrow was to be a joyous yet frightening day, when he left behind childhood, and became a man. His mind wandered back several years, to the parting gift his father had given him as he prepared to leave home. He was going to join an unknown household to begin his long journey into knighthood. As a lowly page he would learn obedience and how to serve, he was a child still, not bold, and found himself yearning for his mother's love and comfort, and was saddened in spirit on that cold morn.

His father had led him into the stable, where, nestling in the straw, lay a newly born colt. "He is yours, in two short years you will return home, and then you both will have much to learn. Train him well for he will become a friend to trust in, on whom your life may depend. We must leave him now, in his mothers care." The young boy knelt by the colt, gently caressing his soft coat, his father looked down on him, struggling to keep back the tears behind his eyes as he remembered his own first parting from home.

When he returned home, a young squire, who must prepare and grow into manhood, he had trained the young colt, calling him Cadair Idris, after the mountain that was tall and strong, yet possessing mystical properties. Now the colt's and his arduous training had come to its end and on the morrow the squire would become a knight. A long vigil awaited him through the coming night, to help him clear his mind, prepare for vows to make, choose his path, be ready to follow where it will take him.

The day began to close, the vigil drew nigh. Rhydian made Cadair's bed, straw piled high, tending to him in his final hours as a child. He took pleasure in the menial task, filling the rick with sweet smelling hay, laying down a deep bed of fresh straw. He then rested, head buried as often before, in the warmth of Cadair's side, leaning against the flank of his horse, aware that tonight his soul would lay strangely bare. His mother had ready a plain, silken shift, white, the symbol of purity, and was now waiting in nervous delight to wash and robe him, to give him water to drink. For today he had fasted, releasing his mind to think. The setting sun cast a rich, fiery, glow as long shadows crept across the castle keep, a slow dark veil falling as he entered the Chapel. Here alone, in this quiet sanctuary, like so many before him, he would spend the long night in contemplation of what will follow, to atone for man's sins, to become a knight, to take his sacred vow.

In the small castle chapel the soft rays of the morning sun slipped through a window, finding the youth, placing a halo round his head. So still he was, like a carved angel, kneeling before the altar, until distant sounds broke the spell, with many raised voices, chanting hymns. Slowly the youth stirred, he stretched his cramped limbs, listening. Surely he heard his name carried on the breeze as the throng drew near?

He felt calm, with a sense of ease that drove away an unnatural fear, he stepped out to await them. There were many visitors from far around gathered on the Castle green. Now was the time for old friends to be found, for new ones to be made. Suddenly a ripple of expectation ran through the crowd - who would make the creation of the new knight? Rumour abounded, for a definate sighting had been made of royal garb, could it be a princeling?

Striding firmly to the green, still in a trancelike bliss, came Rhydian, to all the speculation, as yet, oblivious, only stopping when he reached the appointed place. He caught the eye of his father, his mothers face came into view, he wondered why no one came to greet him, but held back as if in awe. Then out of the dim shadows came a tall figure and he saw the royal dragon of wales blazoned across the shield, a symbol of knightly tales.

A mighty sword, ready to wield, was raised high, held firm in the hand of Prince Llywelyn, whose very word was law throughout the land. His voice rang out strong "Approach me without fright, your time is now, you belong with the chosen few, the right to bear arms and so defend your home, protect the weak, give sustenance and befriend the poor, remaining meek in thought, with spirit free. Son of Cymru, bow before your liege" On bended knee the young man knelt in front of his liege lord. The sword, with a flash of light rested on his shoulder, gently, "Arise Sir Rhydian – I lay claim to you, for you are my knight I command you to follow your conscience and God's light" And so the squire faded into the past as a new Knight entered the tales of lore, to follow the rules of chivalry.

Chapter Two - A Prince's Request

The new knight meditated as calm descended, in the quiet aftermath of the day when all the guests having left, were now making their way home, some to castles, some to cottages, each holding fast to their memories, for they had seen their prince at last.

Many thoughts filled his mind, as ideas chased around in circles, he could find no answers. "What ails you, Sir Rhydian? Tonight you have the right to any lady of your choice. Go have your fill in true delight". Prince Llywelyn laughed at the look of pain upon his newest knight's face as he heard these ribald words. Raising his eyes to his lord's face the young man replied, without flinching. "Last night, at my vigil, I made a vow, in that sacred place; to be a true knight, to honour the code, protect the weak. To serve my Liege and our Lord, carnal pleasures not to seek until true love I find." The Prince looked on this comely youth; there he could see a reflection of himself when young. Llywelyn was silent for a while, "I wish you to join my household, up North, at Castell y Bere. I want you to travel alone, taking the high roads, with only the deer and wolves for company."

He held him there just by the eye, then turning, he walked away. His word was law and with a sigh Sir Rhydian knew that he must follow. Slowly, in his heart, grew a glow of anticipation, for he would play the part of Sir Peredur, a journey, mayhap a quest beckoned, in which to prove himself worthy to call a prince his friend.

As the time for his journey drew nigh Sir Rhydian polished his sword well. He now had his own arms, which his shield bore, a bright blazon, so all could tell what manner of man this knight was. The colour of Or for generosity of spirit, with ordinaries of rich Gules, for strength and magnanimity, his courage, strength and virtue shown by Unicorns, whilst a springing Stag was witness to peace and harmony, with a Harp to bring mystical heaven closer to earth. Under his surcoat he wore no armour, for this quest was not one of battle, but a seeking of inner succor, it's challenge would be to find his true path to travel, with the comforts of home left far behind, taking counsel from none but his own thoughts.

His father called him to his side "Before you go on you path, come with me to choose your guard, companion and friend". Together they went into the stable, where the castles great hounds lay. "You will need protection from the wolves that hide during the day then hunt at night. And from others who hunt in the dark, those men who would take everything you hold dear. Look around; take the strongest, bravest of the pack, one who kills swiftly and silently, one who can follow a cold trail across the rugged hills, for this will keep you safe and well fed"

Heeding these words, Rhydian took measure of every hound, seeking a connection, taking his time, one bitch, the smallest there, returned his gaze without fear or submission. Gently he called to her; quietly she rose, and stood by his side. He rested his hand on her head. "This is my dog, in whom I will trust. Her name shall be Cyfaill."

His father seemed rather troubled "I hope you have chosen well, for this dog is not the strongest of the pack." With a smile Rhydian replied "I am satisfied that her heart is brave, I know it is true that, like me, she is yet untried, so we will learn together" Then as the sun rose up in the sky Sir Rhydian mounted Cadair,

and with his hound running behind, he rode out of
Castell Du, to begin his quest, his noble deed.

Chapter Three - The Journey Begins

From the distant castle tower his mother watched him depart, sending prayers upon the wind. She felt a deep sorrow within in her heart, for her only child, her son, was all alone, about make an arduous journey, to follow the wild forbidding mountain path. She spoke gently, no one there to hear her "Why leave me behind, to seek your fortune? This fair castle is a forlorn place without your laughter, without your smiles, without the light that shines from your face, radiating from within and lighting the dark corners when darkness falls. I cannot bear the times to come, for who now will honour me with their presence, bringing me stories of deeds of daring from afar? But most of all, who will protect you, keep you from crossing the final bar?"

For her gallant son, in high excitement, no such worries disturbed the pleasure of riding on a fine day, the warm sun on his back. To have time, the leisure to think in peace, of unbroken silence, except for the natural sounds that amongst men were so often drowned by loud voices, raised in anger. The desire for quiet had set him apart when training, both as a page and squire, now he could listen to the river flowing over rocks, doves cooing in the trees, leaves swaying, with the wind blowing across the long grass beside the banks.

Cadair, eager to go, began to prance, jolting Rhydian back to the present with a rude awakening to his trance. The sudden movement unseated him, and he landed on the ground next to Cyfaill, who, thinking this was a fine game, ran around with glee, her great paws splashing mud on his hose, the same on surcoat. Cadair, saddle slipping, reins entangled, stood close by. With laughter welling up inside he remounted, then letting Cadair fly faster and faster they went along the river banks, running for joy. No longer a solemn knight, just a horse, a hound and a boy.

Their wild headlong charge gradually slowed to a gentle pace as they followed the river, the light reflecting on the water, the waves creating a distorted image of the sun as it crept onwards until it was high in the sky above them, they found a resting place by a wide curve in the bank, where the grass sloped to the edge. Leaving his clothes to dry he washed himself in the river, revelling in the cold water, swimming to the stony bed as he had done so many times before, hands scrabbling among the reeds, with silent laughter he watched as the tiny creatures he disturbed fled from him, so quickly they sped by he could only glimpse the silver flash of bodies against the dark bed, until gasping for breath he burst to the surface, before diving under the water again and again until his body tired of the game and there, in a grassy fold, he fell asleep, with Cyfaill and Cadair, keeping watch.

He dreamt of Uther Pendragon, of Myrddin and the witch Morgain. Tales of yore were taking him to the magic kingdom at Caerleon where Arthur held court. Suddenly he was woken by a random sound, senses alert he cast his eyes around him. What caused his sleep to be upset? The sound came again, close by, yet Cadair and Cyfaill stayed quiet, and seemed to be unconcerned by any noise. As Rhydian looked towards a small stream that bubbled over the rocks into the big river he saw a young girl, all alone singing softly.

Still in the thralls of his dream he wondered if she was Nimue, slowly he walked towards her, and softly he sang too. Their voices mingling in perfect harmony, with words he did not understand, that flowed unbidden from his lips as if learnt a long time ago he gazed deep into her blue eyes, as she, turning, faced him. She gave a mighty cry of laughter, making Rhydian stop in puzzlement, until the truth dawned on him of why the romantic time had passed. With his face turning crimson he fled back to his friends, and hastily donned his clothes once more.

Chapter Four - A Dream

With modesty regained he returned to find the maiden, but the stream where she had sat was empty. With a heavy laden heart he searched all around, calling through the dappled trees that lined the riverside. His could hear the sound of her voice circling inside his mind, the smile in her bright blue eyes seemed to follow him, daring him to find her again. Sadly he called Cyfaill and remounted Cadair, once more journeying westwards towards an unknown future.

He felt sure that one day their paths would cross again, so with youthful optimism and his spirits raised he rode towards a deserted castle where wild herds of cattle now grazed. Here he had played with boyhood friends and became in those games the heroes of legend and myth whose exploits had ensured their names lived on in poetry and song. He wandered beneath the walls of earth where now only the grass grew. From deep within him, a tribal memory, he heard the calls of wounded men and frightened women, the sound of arrows whistling overhead and swords clashing, with the caws of carrion crows waiting in the anticipation of a feast. A shiver came over him; a cold mist was descending into the valley, swirling and beginning to enfold the three companions, the hills appeared to be floating in a sea of cloud.

Close by an old road led upwards, straight as the trunk of a rowan tree, taking the travellers away from ancient battle scenes, to new places as yet undiscovered. As Rhydian left this valley behind, Cadair began to fret, wanting to climb higher, Cyfaill too felt the desire to leave the mist behind. They followed the track to the bare tops of the hills, where the trees thinned out and shelter became hard to find. At the summit, as the sun began to set, he cast around for a place to camp among bare, odd, shapes, roughly marked out by stonewalls that had lost their purpose, dislodged and strewn in random places. With damp clinging to their clothes he could find no means of making a fire to keep them dry and safe from attackers. Feeling lost, almost afraid, emotions deep within rose to the surface and he sank to the ground. A warm muzzle rested itself on his knee as Cyfaill laid herself beside him, Cadair, lifted his head to watch, before grazing quietly, and he felt comforted, like a child protected, and so Sir Rhydian slept.

Just before dawn he was roused from his slumber, not yet awake he stayed very still. As he watched, orderly rows of soldiers passed him by, the rhythmic sound of marching feet seemed to shake the ground and echo inside his head, with a constant beat. They were clad in strange uniforms, the like of which he had never seen before, behind them came sweating horses, pulling small carts. Keen to see more, Rhydian crept closer; he looked in surprise at the scene that lay before his eyes. Here were high walls and buildings where there had been none the night before. He could hear calls across the hills, in a strange yet familiar language.

He looked in vain for Cadair and Cyfaill but they had vanished, he was all alone and fear gripped his being, he began to pray and wished he too could disappear. A soldier went by, so close he almost touched him, yet he remained unseen, as if he was indeed invisible. Rhydian crossed himself, as a dim recollection of stories long since heard, about soldiers from a distant land, sweeping through Cymru, devastating the countryside with a heavy hand. They had left buildings and forts behind, with broad roads such as the one he had ridden from Tre'rcastell to here. He could hear two men talking, and found that some of the words spoken he could understand, sensing feelings of great excitement and many plots afoot.

As the sun rose and dawn broke over the hillside the troops simply melted away, the buildings, the horses, all were no more, just the wide open space, with Cadair quietly grazing and Cyfaill, twitching, still chasing coneys in her sleep. He pondered, had it been only a dream? Searching around by where the soldiers had stood, his sharp eyes spotted an old coin. He picked it up and gently rubbed the earth from it, as he did so a gleam of yellow metal shone through and there on one side, in proud relief, was a face, with leaves encircling its head, numbers and words faintly showing, but not so clearly that he could read them. Trying to recall the words he had heard spoken, he thought hard, what had those soldiers said? There had been one word that he surely knew - aurum - gold!

Chapter Five - A Change Of Plan

Pondering on last night's events, Rhydian made his way down the hillside, with Cadair picking his way down a path so steep, he began to slip and slide, his great hooves were not built for mountain ways, yet still he took good care of his charge. Gradually the going grew softer as the scrub began to give way to fields of lush grass with clear water to drink from. Refreshing themselves they made their way to the distant river, looking for a place to cross. Far to the west Rhydian saw a castle rising above the flat land, an encampment of many men and horses moving below the great earth embankments.

Warily he moved northwards, as memories of tales told on dark nights around the fires of home came unbidden to his imagination. How hoards of English soldiers fought the Lord Rhys, to recapture this castle the stronghold of a Norman knight. When Lord Rhys died his sons had continued to fight, for whoever held the fort had command of this valley, at the meeting of three rivers. And so it still remained, a place of unceasing conflict, with squabbles of ownership and rights continuing.

Rhydian forded the nearest of these rivers, Cadair had no need to swim, his height kept the rider dry, as he strode with ease along the river bed, Cyfaill was in danger of being taken by the current, now swelled with the recent mountain rain, her slim body shivered. Rhydian leant down, and holding fast to the scruff of her neck he pulled her onto the pommel of his saddle, which being made to fit a knight in full armour comfortably, gave plenty of room for a youth and his hound. Cadair arched his neck and with pride he carried his friends safely to the other bank. Once across Rhydian began to look for shelter should he need to hide from the men, he noticed the same stone shapes as last night, with stone walls laid out in square patterns. From here rough tracks led towards the North West, in parts covered by spare grass but without a doubt it was a roadway.

In the way he had learnt when a squire, Rhydian gathered sticks, moss and dry bark, which he placed on a roughly built stone hearth, ready to make a fire. He hobbled Cadair, took a small silk net out of his pack and calling to Cyfaill, headed for the river. In a quiet backwater he set his trap, Cyfaill watched, then joyfully she bounded through the water, with silver drops splashing behind. Brown backed fish, with the sunlight flashing along their sleek sides, startled by her presence, darted into the shelter of the rocks, unaware of the net spread out beneath them. Swiftly Rhydian lifted the net, and with its opening closed tight, dinner was caught.

Careful not to let any smoke betray their presence Rhydian cooked the fish, offering some to Cyfaill, who looking disdainfully at this, lazily arose and disappeared into the long grass, soon returning with her own skillfully caught dinner, for she by far preferred coney to fish. As he ate Rhydian thought hard, his plan had been to follow the river, but now there was a need to avoid the castle. Rhydian looked longingly at the track, a sliver of stone cutting a straight furrow, beckoning him to follow. He recalled last night dream soldiers; surely they would have taken this route? His mind made up, knowing he was right, he resumed his journey, not the easy way along the river, but following the half hidden track onto the wild moor.

Firstly they had to cross the flood plain between the three rivers, which offered no shelter; Rhydian rode fast across it, keeping far to the north of the castle. Reaching the last and biggest of the rivers they rested on the moss covered stones of its bank. He looked out at the fast flowing current then touching his friend he spoke gently, "Cadair Idris, you needs must be as strong as your namesake to carry us safely through the water, I put my trust in you." Then, with Cyfaill once more on the saddle with him, they rode straight into the foaming water, with steady purpose Cadair bore his load over the river.

Suddenly the big horse paused, with nostrils flaring, and his head held high, causing Cyfaill to quiver. Rhydian listened to the wind, a soft sigh seemed to be caressing him, pulling his gaze downwards to the river bed where the bright stones, shimmered, changing shape, into blue eyes, framed by long dark hair. The sound of music swirled inside his head, bewitching him with a voice of such rare purity, that it was not of mortals, but enticing him to sink deep beneath the waves, filling his young soul with the desire to follow, to join in the eternal song. Then the spell broke, leaving a fire, smouldering forever, in his heart.

Cadair, once more able to move, reached the far side, leaping up the bank he took off down the old track, not stopping until the river with its sprite was far behind, Cyfaill running as if the devil were chasing her out of hell. The desperate race gradually slowing down as their panic grew less, until, hidden from sight they found a grassy hollow to stop. Drawing deep breaths of air, and now feeling shamed by his fearful flight, Rhydian dismounted from his sweating horse. With Cyfaill's body pressing against his side he took handfuls of grass and with rhythmic strokes dried his destrier. Feeling pride in the powerful muscles and glossy coat, with each steady sweep he regained control

19

of his own fears. A smile crept across his face, fired by memories of eyes, deep as the pool where Tylwyth dwelt, framed by jet black witches' hair that curled upwards, eyes set in a timeless face. For although it may belong in the realms of myth and legend, yet his sprite was still of this time and this place.

The friends needed to rest and eat; here was lush grass, with game a plenty to hunt and a fresh leat to drink from, a perfect place to stay. Rhydian lit a fire which cast its shadows all around, now at peace, music filled his mind, as the evocative sound of her voice entered into his soul, from where he took the notes, weaving them together, creating a symphony of song which swelled inside him until he too was singing. Softly at first, until increasing in power, echoes rebounded off the hillsides, chasing each other, notes repeating in a never ending canon that rode across the valley in joyful praise. Finally, all passion spent, he slept like an innocent babe, unknowing that those who had heard his song had wept.

Chapter Six - The Old Road

The morning sun slipped over the gorse, casting a rosy hue over the sleeping youth lying curled around his hound, with his horse quietly grazing quietly nearby, yet watchful of his charge. As the rays touched Rhydian's face he began to stir, stretching his lithe body he reached out to his friends, his hand stroking Cyfaill's head, then calling to Cadair, he prepared to continue the journey. His eyes swept ahead, seeking trace of the old track as it headed straight over the highland, a faint thread, but for those who looked, a certain sign to follow. All day long they travelled, at peace with the world. They drank water from streams, keeping well fed with game hunted by skill and guile.

For one day more they rode the track until the path led down the hillside. Here the land seemed strange, with black scars that cut through shrubs, large flat areas, steep sides, like a giant stairway winding round in a spiral towards a large pit surrounded by bare rock, vainly trees and plants struggled to gain a foothold in this land. Casting around, Rhydian sought a sheltered place to sleep in the waste tips of this disturbed ground where haunted souls seemed to remain.

He had not slept for long when low sounds woke him, voices from above drifting on the air. Figures in the glow of a flaming torch moved toward him, closer they came, until he could hear them speak in that same strangely familiar language he had heard before, then, clear and loud he heard the word he knew "Aurum" He watched the two climb upwards, past other figures that lay sleeping until they reached a rocky outcrop, then disappeared, so fast that Rhydian lost them from sight. Far below the land had changed, no trees to be seen, just soil, well dug, piled high onto earthy heaps. Mist began to swirl around, a clammy coil entwining Rhydian, as if an invisible hand reached across him, blocking the scene from view. Unable to see further he returned back to his camp, to ponder on what it could mean.

The next morning he tethered Cadair to a low tree, and keeping Cyfaill right beside him he headed for the place where he had lost the two men from sight. As he reached the rocky wall, the ground under his feet suddenly gave way, and he was falling, down into a cold, dank hole, where no sunlight could play. He reached the bottom, landing heavily, and lay there, winded. Cyfaill howled in fear, the sound echoing down to him. Standing up, he stretched out and found he was unable to reach the top. He felt the wall of stone, smooth as glass, cold and slippery, with centuries of moss growing, there was no handhold here.

Missing nothing Rhydian ran his hands everywhere, until he found one stone, much bigger than the rest, which in texture felt different, rougher to the touch. He tried to move it, digging his fingers along its edge, with excitement increasing he gradually pulled the whole stone forward. Taking his dagger, he gouged at the stone sides until it came right away, revealing a small cavity in the wall. Reaching deep down he felt something wet and cold, resting on the bottom, covered in slime and feeling very heavy, he pulled out an old leather pouch. Tucking this inside his jerkin, he tried to climb out, using his dagger he made crevices in the wall, scraping the crumbling mortar between the stones, hoping to gain some foothold, but to no avail. With no one to help, his hopes began to fade, he thought of home, of his parents waiting in vain for news of his travels. He thought of his beloved Cadair, of Cyfaill, who it seemed, had left him in peril, to rot in this forgotten Oubliette.

Just when hope had died away he heard sounds, getting closer, afraid to call out, he began to pray. As if in answer Cyfaill's loud baying rang out, then something wet touched his hand. Rhydian caught hold of a silken rope, feeling the rope tighten and take the strain as Cadair pulled back, Rhydian scrambled out. A joyous hound, looking very pleased with herself, covered him in wet licks, flecked with blood.

As Rhydian released the rope, he saw it was Cadair's tether, chewed through by Cyfaill so working together they could rescue their beloved friend. Feeling shame that he had so quickly doubted her, he marvelled at his hound, saying, "I put my trust in both of you, strength and stamina I have from Cadair, beauty and brains are your gift to me. What can I give back? My solemn promise that forever you have my heart and loyalty". Then in quiet companionship the trio continued on their way, with a humbler Sir Rhydian than first had left Castell Du, learning much as he journeyed further.

Walking down the mountain side they passed several streams, very straight, with stony sides. This caused Rhydian to ponder, likening them to the mill leats at home, but there were no mills here to be seen. Along each course were pools, becoming broader, then narrowing again until they joined the meandering river. Soon they reached water meadows, with lush green grass for Cadair, coneys for Cyfaill to chase, and the sun's warmth to entice a weary, chastened, traveller to stay in this serene place.

Placing all their belongings on the ground, Rhydian sat down to rest, he took out the leather pouch, and gently drew from it a small lump of metal, covered in earth, then more lumps, some very large. Lastly he brought out a circlet, with a round stone, rather dull, in the middle. Curious he took them to the water, washing the mud away, until a brightness began to show, a sudden dart of gold as the finely wrought circlet caught the sunlight, reflected it back, with blue fire dancing and shimmering from deep within the stones heart.

As he held it out over the river, he saw the sprites lovely face again; the circlet appeared to nestle in her black hair, her eyes, the same blue as the jewel, opened wide with delight. He could hear laughter on the wind, but he felt no surprise only a sense of belonging, as if he was looking at a part of himself, the kindred soul of a long known friend. He gazed down into the water, their eyes meeting in mutual recognition, then slowly the face faded away leaving its imprint burned on his mind.

Chapter Seven - An Old Man

Rhydian left Cadair free to graze, with no more need of tether or hobble, certain he would stay waiting for him. Calling Cyfaill he took his sling, silken net and dagger to hunt for supper. The woods near by beckoned with promise of a different kind of game to seek. The trees closed around him, with many animal tracks crossing his path, then, in excitement, he saw it, the boar's unique print, stealthily he followed the trail, sure signs of a group with young. Suddenly Cyfaill stood still, with ears pricked and nose quivering, she darted off into the dense bushes. Curious, Rhydian went after, her way clearly marked; this was unusual, for she was well trained to be a quiet hunter who left little trace. He heard her call to him, urgently, quickening his pace he found her at a small entrance set into the side of the hill. Warily he looked in, bent almost double he saw that it opened out, into a cavern, with light coming in from above, whilst a large hound, hackles raised, stood guard.

Cyfaill entered the tunnel, Rhydian, taking out his dagger crept after her. He watched her as she circled the walls, finding it hard to keep still, but trusting her instincts, he waited. The great dog let her come close, then with tail lifting high he allowed Rhydian to move forward, there he saw movement in the dim recesses and heard a low sigh. As his eyes grew accustomed to the dim light he made out the figure of an old man, lying on a pile of rags. Using soft words he drew closer, soothing the hound with his calm voice until he reached the bed. Under the crumbled blankets a face, such as an ancient bard, stared up at him on which he noted many lines, etched by pain. A long grey beard was set below a long narrow nose, unfocused eyes of a brighter blue than he had ever seen, looked at him, they seemed much younger than the face they dwelt in, yet so old and wise.

Kneeling beside the old man Rhydian put his hand on the brow, which felt hot, but dry as if there was a fever still to break. He took a cloth and soaked it from the clear water that ran from a spring in a corner of the cave. Willing the old man to speak, he bathed his face and trickled drops of water into his mouth. He stripped back the bedding, as he had seen his mother do, then he wiped the old man's bony body, freshening and cooling it. He saw the eyes begin to focus on him, and from the face a new light glowed. The eyes closed and the old man fell into a natural sleep. For the next five days and long nights Rhydian tended to the old man, keeping him dry, warm and well fed, only leaving the cave to hunt with Cyfaill and visit Cadair.

As his health began to be restored by the care given to him by this stranger, the old man watched from his bed and wondered about the youth. He began asking questions of him, seeking to find the truth, and receiving back a true account, then answers from him were sought. In quiet companionship they talked throughout the nights until on the sixth day they parted, to follow their separate ways.

"Sir Rhydian of Castell Du I bid you farewell, these days together have brought me joy, I know that we will meet again for our fates are surely entwined, you cared for me without gain. I am known by many different names, but should you have need of me ask for Emrys. I give you tokens, you can be sure that my friends will honour you for bearing these."

Holding the old man in his arms Rhydian felt a power, like a hot bolt that sped between them, curling

26

around his very soul. With tears unshed he turned and left, Cyfaill followed behind, saddened to leave Cabal, the wolfhound. Once more reunited with Cadair they journeyed on, bound northward along the river's edge, with Rhydian finding there was an empty space now lying in his heart, where an old man had claimed a place.

They crossed the river by the old bridge, where Cadair, eager to go after his long rest, raced across, giving Rhydian no time to linger by the water, hoping for yet one more sight of his water sprite, afraid lest she was there, yet afraid she was gone for evermore. The early morning sun lit up the path ahead, like an arrow its course was straight, partly hidden as it climbed out of the valley to the hills above, where it made a visible scar; a white road over the wild moorland.

Into this remote land they travelled, far from any settlement, with nothing to guide them but the sun by day and at night the stars. Rhydian thought of the old man and his parting gifts, with love and delight. A cup and ring, made from the same blue-flecked stone, carved with an ancient sign. He recalled the words spoken as they had parted.

"Wear the ring to show you are my friend, drink from the cup if you are in malign health or injured, for it has the power to cure both the body and the soul if the user is a true believer in its worth and uses it power wisely with no thought of gain. My last gift to you is a simple crwth and bow, care for it well; it was made from the thorn tree of Aramethea. The music it plays will heal a troubled spirit, bring comfort to the grieving and remove fear from all who hear it, play it well, for my sake."

They journeyed on for two days, along the high road, at night Rhydian sang as he played the crwth, with music flowing so freely, as if released by the bow from long captivity. On the second day they came down from the hills to a wide valley, with small houses scattered alongside the river. As he approached, children came out to see the stranger and admire his horse and hound. Pointing at his crwth they chanted Sing, Sing. Smiling, Rhydian began to play, and as his voice gathered in strength the hills began to sing back.

The three companions continued the next day having sung and talked until the early hours of the morning, then, on sweet smelling hay they slept 'til long past the dawn breaking. Taking with him new songs and tales Rhydian once more travelled northwards, his mind busy with the music and fables of last night. As the sun rose high in the sky he began to feel warm and drowsy, he stopped at a quiet spot, where lying down on the grass, was soon sleeping.

He was woken by Cyfaill, a low growl shaking her body. Sitting on the river bank was a slim figure, with long black hair falling down her back. As he watched, his eyes sank into her beauty; slowly he arose and walked towards her. As he drew close she raised her hand to stop him. "Come no further, for the time is not yet right" Then as he gazed a mist arose from the water, shrouding her from view. It cleared and she was gone, in silence she had came and in silence she had left. He searched for signs, but there were none, sadly he mounted and continued along the path.

Chapter Eight - Aldan

They continued alongside the river until nightfall, making camp inside one of many ruined buildings with grass growing between stone walls. Rhydian looked across the river to a small village, dominated by a church that sat on the top of a low mound. He remembered the stories told to him only yesterday, of the place St David had preached, where he found the skill of oration that lifted him above all others. The Archbishop's crown was given to him there, at Brefi.

That night dreams returned to Rhydian, awakening him as the moon shone over the land. He could see no ruins, but now a fort stood in its place, soldiers, in full regalia, stood guard along the battlements. He looked for his two friends, but they had vanished. With a growing sense of awe and wonderment he drew nearer. A horseman rode past, so close he could feel the air stir around him, but there were no sounds, no voices, no hooves clattering over the flagstones, a deathly silence, so profound it could almost be heard.

A sudden movement came from behind him, turning he saw two men pushing a young, frightened, girl to the ground. Without a second thought, dagger in his hand, Sir Rhydian charged, ready to battle for the maiden's honour. He ran straight through them, making no contact, the figures wavered, as if blown by a waft of air, the girl broke free, running fast. Slow to react the two men could not catch her, in bad humour they returned to the fort. The girl turned round a puzzled look in her deep blue eyes, long hair, black as the night, framed her face. Rhydian frowned for she was his water sprite, yet could not see him. As he stood watching, the dawn broke, sweeping away the fort, the girl, the soldiers. Once more Rhydian could see Cadair and Cyfaill, still sleeping peacefully amongst the broken, ruined walls.

Rhydian looked to the hills beyond the ruins, where the old road marched on, straight as a lance, heading northwards. He had followed this track for many miles, yet now he felt a strange reluctance to follow the same route any more. With a new sense of purpose he took the pathway down to the river ford and crossed over into the village, finding the place where St David had come to deliver his oration against the heretics, the followers of Pelagius. On reaching the small hill he climbed up to the church and entered with a sense of awe and reverence.

Approaching the half timbered chancel he could feel a passion trapped within its very walls, closing his eyes, he opened his mind, willing the spirit shadows to reveal their secrets. In stillness he listened across the centuries, hoping to find answers to, as yet, unformed and unasked questions. The cool dim interior seemed to be bathed in light; the silence was broken by an angelic voice, softly at first then growing louder. To the new young knight it felt as if his soul was being lifted by the beauty of a sound that was both strange yet well known.

As he slowly turned to face the source, it all faded away, leaving not a note behind, as if blown by the mountain breeze, scattered into the air. Yet there did remain a trace, a glowing ember, hidden deep, warming his being from within, for it was the very essence of life. Feeling humbler yet uplifted, he left the church and rode towards the village green. Here people were selling their wares, cloth, bread, chickens in cages, pens with piglets, squealing loudly as children poked them with sticks laughing, as they fled from side to side.

Rhydian looked with longing at the loaves, realising how boring a diet of fish and coney can be.

He picked up his cwrth and began to play, ballads and love songs that flowed as sweet as honey. As a crowd gathered around him he started singing, his voice at first caressing, soft and gentle, gradually rising in strength to a final, soaring crescendo, reaching to all those listening, even across the valley. There was a moment of silence when he finished, then a mighty wave of applause, coins were tossed at his feet and he was almost swept along the street by the throng of admirers. Still smiling, he crossed to the baker's stand, now with money to buy plenty. As he wandered around the market he heard barking from the green, turning, he saw one man with raised stick aimed at Cyfaill, another man, with Cadair's reins, trying to lead him away. Rhydian shouted in great anger and ran straight at them. With a parting kick at the hound the men disappeared.

"Your fine horse can be a great temptation, you need to guard him well; these parts are a thieves den" A pair of bright blue eyes looked at Rhydian, for a moment his heart leapt, but the face they were set in was older than his maiden from last night. Her black hair was flecked with grey, her figure yet still trim, and the stare colder. "If you are travelling alone keep to the open road and trust no one" Rhydian, thanking her for the advice, asked her name.

"I am called Aldan, I see you are wearing the ring of Emrys, for that, I will give you help" Saying no more she passed him, entering a small house on the edge of the village. Rhydian thought carefully, for his Cadair was a noble destrier and that could not be hidden. He must take care now he was travelling along well used routes. He would keep watch and as he had been bidden trust no one. With a heavy heart he continued on his way.

Part Two

In
Friendship

Chapter Nine - An Unexpected Companion

Rhydian took the valley road out of Brefi; other travellers were also journeying, with goods and livestock, both in company and alone. Keeping a good distance behind them he rode thoughtfully along, wondering which pathway to follow. Should he take the gentle low road? It was much frequented, with all the fears that might bring, or once more to take the high ground, to the hills where the very wildness itself brought danger. It was not far to the next settlement, and the sun was warm on his back, the river road more pleasant than climbing to the sparse moor lands above and so he continued along the easier byway.

He lunched by the water, idly throwing stones for Cyfaill, thinking of the tales he had heard, of old crones, wizards and enchantresses, of daring deeds and stories from days past. He then weaved these into songs, strumming his crwth creating melodies, softly singing them until he believed they were worthy to be heard. Now decided on his course he continued once more along the road, passing through the next village without halting until he came to where the valley broadened out, here where once a lake had been, a vast bog stretched in front of him.

Watchful of his step he kept in the lee of the hills, on firmer ground. Rising above the bog were small hillocks, as if dragons slept amidst a cauldron of mire. Not trusting the ground beneath him, Cadair trod carefully, picking his way along ancient paths. That night they heard strange eerie calls, spirit fires dancing, Ellylldan's at play.

Morning broke; waking Rhydian from restless slumber, all around was peaceful, layers of mist hanging like a blanket over the land. A rustle in the reeds caused him to turn quickly, there lying in a small dyke, was a boy, with black hair and deep blue eyes, a face so familiar to Rhydian he felt no surprise at finding him in this remote place. Offering his hand he pulled the urchin out, and surveyed his prize.

"Tell me, son of Aldan, why you have followed me, and what your name is?" the boy stared at Rhydian, "How do you know who I am? My name is Alain, my mother charged me with tracking you, keeping myself hidden, to watch for any danger until it was safe to show myself – but I fell into the bog and now you will send me home" He looked shamed, but stood tall and straight, and although his eyes began to fill his gaze did not waver. "Your eyes told me who you are, your courage too. If you wish to come with me a while I will be glad of you company." The boy flushed with pride, then he drew from inside his coat a parcel, which he gave to Rhydian. "This is a gift for you, from my mother" Rhydian opened the soft, light parcel revealing a blanket woven from fine yarn, in many shades of blue, from the grey-blue of mist to the deep blue of night, it seemed to shimmer in the sunlight capturing the warmth and reflecting its light. His hands felt a glow spreading over his body.

"My mother sends this to keep you from any chilling of the spirit, as well as keeping the cold at bay; you will be refreshed whenever you use this for cover. An hour's sleep will be as a full night. She has only woven one other" Feeling its touch, gentle as a lover, Rhydian was overcome. "She gave this to me, a stranger?" Alain smiled, "She said you were known to her, how I have no knowledge." Twisting Emrys' ring he knew this was truth, a thread bound them and he made a vow that before his journey ended he would seek the answer.

The sun climbed in the sky, burning the mist from the land, and over the river, as it meandered through its flood plain, a lonely scene, stretching as far as Rhydian could see. On all sides, as the flat peat mire ended, mountains rose steeply upwards, with the sun's reflected rays creating a circle of fire. Shadowy demons chased across the valley, fading into the dawning light. He was reluctant to leave, for magical spirits graced this place and there was a sense of belonging, as if he had been here before. He knew the ways, untold, he knew how to avoid the deep quaking pits, where to tread to find the solid ground beneath his feet, with old understanding, passed to him from lives gone by.

Alain looked expectantly at him, unsure of his place, ready to go, he almost quivered with excitement. Rhydian smiled as he looked at the eager young face, "It seems I have acquired a squire of my own, strange, for only a few days since, that was my role." They travelled slowly, for Cadair found the way hard, sinking in the moss he struggled to gain control in the marsh, using his great strength he forced a pathway through. Cyfaill found the going easy she seemed to glide over the reed beds, leaving no trace behind.

Turning eastwards, under the lee of the hills, where the ground rose higher, a track took them safely over the land. Here were manmade workings, where peat had been dug out for the fires of the small dwellings scattered along the edge, on the hillside, each with their own clearings, making patchworks of green set among the brown.

Alain spoke to Rhydian, "Ahead is a town with fairs where many visit, they have jugglers and games. I come here, with my mother, who sells her wares, I earn coins by holding horses and running errands" In truth, now he had two to feed and sorely needed bread. Looking at the boy's face, with his bright blue eyes shining, he could not gainsay him, laughing he said "As my squire you must only attend to my horse." At this Rhydian vaulted up onto Cadair's broad back, pulling Alain up behind him, they left Cors Carron's treacherous paths to follow the white monks' track. In high humour they rode into the small town, passing other travellers on their way to the fair.

Alain led them to an Inn where he was known; there he sought shelter from the cool night air in the warm dry stable loft, as so often before. Rhydian settled Cadair on fresh straw, filled the rick with sweet smelling hay, and left him with Cyfaill for company. Alain watched; keen to be quick to learn his new duties. The cobbled square was already taking on a festive air, with at its centre, a Celtic stone cross marking the site where the fair stalls would be placed. In a field adjacent brightly coloured flags fluttered from poles, and in the middle was a raised dais, whilst at the far end, a row of butts was being erected. Looking around Rhydian felt a wave of excitement beginning to grow inside him, for this was no ordinary village fair, but a gathering of many people from far and wide.

The pair returned to the Inn full of the sights with much to ask Alain's friends. In past visits here, Alain had worked as a pot boy, paying for his nights lodging, but with two hungry boys, a horse and dog this was no longer enough. The Innkeeper, seeing Rhydian's crwth, asked him what manner of songs he played, he did not want monkish chants or lovesick ballads, his guests tastes were for an altogether more bawdy fare! Alain washed and Rhydian sung for their keep that night, until they tumbled into their beds tired, but happy, ready for a good night's sleep to prepare themselves for the morrows fair.

Chapter Ten - Fair Day

In the early morning light, Rhydian crept quietly down to the stable, not wishing to disturb his new friend. With only a halter he rode Cadair away from the town, no one had yet risen, the only sounds to be heard were those of animals in their pens and of vermin scuttling through the deserted streets. They cantered through the water meadows; beneath him Rhydian could feel the horse stretching himself, enjoying freedom after a night indoors. As people began to stir, he turned back to the Inn, where he found Alain had prepared a fresh straw bed for Cadair, and with Cyfaill's head on his knee, sat by a newly cleaned saddle, proud in his new role. Rhydian gathered up all their possessions, which he carefully stowed in a corner of the stable, well hidden in the straw.

With the crwth slung over his shoulder, leaving the horse and hound behind, they strode out of the courtyard, and made for the market where many tradesmen were setting up stalls, hassling for the best places, with bartering amongst themselves already begun. They bought marchpane and honey sweetmeats from a peddler, washed down with a cup of beer. They turned to the tourney field, where preparations were underway for the combat games. A loud jeer from behind caused him to turn, and saw a group of men, laughing at him and pointing to his crwth. "Sing us a love song, pretty boy, we are wrestlers, travelled from Kernow, to win prizes, a youth such as you, with golden hair and soft white skin can pleasure us, if no maidens can be found"

Feeling anger rise inside him, though struggling to keep calm, Rhydian passed them, not a sound did he

41

utter, instead he headed for the booths and placed his name to all the lists, taking part in every game, from quarter staves and archery to stone pitching and tug o'war, then, his heart racing, he added his mark to the main attraction.

With still some hours before the games started the two wandered around the fair, mingling with the jugglers. In the square Rhydian started to sing, a crowd collected, and as they listened to him silence fell. People stopped their work until he finished singing, then they resumed, spirits uplifted, pockets lighter, the beauty of his voice still ringing in their ears. A band marched through to the fair ground, leading the Drummers, a small dancing dog twirled to his piper as they wended their way to the games. A hand cart, carrying the greased hog was pushed by a small boy, who puffed his way to the field. Rhydian attached himself to the rear of this motley crew, Alain, carrying the crwth, followed, his excitement tinged with a fear that his new friend might have overstepped himself.

Once on the field Rhydian found the tents, to prepare himself for the tasks ahead. Alain counted his money; there was plenty for the side shows. First he bet clipped pence at the cock pit, he climbed the greasy pole, chased the greased pig, and threw horseshoes at rings. His cock won and he caught the pig, he slithered up the pole, seeming unable to lose, his pile of pennies grew. Gleefully he went to the Archery Butts to watch as Rhydian started his games.

Many years of practise had given him true flight, finding the bullseye with repeated shafts. The fighting with staves had an extra part, taking place on a large log, balanced over a muddy pond. Roars of laughter could be heard, for whenever one of those fighting lost their balance, they fell into the quagmire. Being quite light and lithe this was one sport Rhydian had loved as a boy, his nimble feet and natural balance kept him steady as he fought all comers. As he progressed around the field his support grew, until he reached the centre, where the Cornish wrestlers waited for him. Alain looked at the slight figure of his mentor measuring up against his burly opponents. A great fear gnawed away at his inside for he was sorely afraid that Rhydian would be hurt, injured, perhaps maimed for life, or worse, and all for the sake of an injured pride.

The bouts took place until only two men were left standing, Rhydian and the biggest, strongest of the men who had taunted him. As they circled each other the crowd became still. Holding tight to loose linen tunics, each tried to pull the other down. Experience versus youth, a solid rock against acrobatics.

Unable to hold this slippery adversary for long, with patience being tried by quick sharp kicks, the wrestler's temper began to rise, tiring, he dropped his guard. Swiftly and using an unexpected strength, Rhydian attacked. The older man hit the ground and there he stayed, unable to rise within the allotted time, with head bowed he submitted, and so relinquished his crown. Rising to its feet the cheering crowd gave homage to a new Champion.

Chapter Eleven - The Aftermath

With the cheers of the crowd ringing in his ears Rhydian felt himself being lifted up, high in the air onto the broad shoulders of the men from Kernow, who paraded him around the field, with not a thought nor a care for the loser. They stripped the borrowed wrestling tunic from his lithe body, leaving him bare to the waist, creating lustful pleasure among the young maids, with older ones wishing that the years had not hastened them by so quickly, whilst unnoticed in this heady excitement, the defeated man slipped from the ground.

After some time the victor and his squire left the fair, Alain carrying a squealing, greasy, piglet, fat and round; for Rhydian, the winner's purse and a linen tunic given to him as a memento of this day. Neither saw the movement behind them, a shadowy figure, keeping distance, following them, watching which way they went. At the Inn they checked on Cadair, a gentle whinny greeting them, they released Cyfaill from her long wait, and then promising to return very soon, went into the Inn. A figure silently entered the stable, eyes alight with hate, and bent on revenge, he saw a richer prize than he had lost; softly he approached Rhydian's beloved horse.

The Inn was very noisy with revelers packed inside, beer flowed freely, tales told, becoming increasingly coarse. Cyfaill suddenly sprang up, hackles raised, barking loudly. Rhydian followed across the yard; with pounding heart he reached the stall, where Cadair stood still, nostrils flaring, eyes staring, sweat breaking out down his neck, legs braced apart. In the gloom, slumped against the wall, with blood pouring from his head, his breathing laboured, uneven, all colour drained away, lay the defeated wrestler.

Rhydian bent down and gently moved him. It was then he saw the damaged leg, badly smashed and twisted. Calling for Alain to fetch his saddle pack, he withdrew Emrys' cup, filling it with water from Cadair's trough, he bathed the head wound. The ice cold water grew warmer as it touched the skin, inducing a healing sleep to settle on the injured man, then covering him in Aldan's blanket Rhydian, worried, left him to sleep. "I can care for his head wound, but his broken limb is beyond my knowledge. The monks at Ystrad Fflur can tend him well, so tonight I must take him there"

Alain started to argue, he could not understand why this man should not be left, why this concern and care for a thief. Looking stern Rhydian replied "Judge no man for we are no better than our fellows. I have vowed to serve all those in need and in this I will not falter" Alain was much humbled by these words, and felt proud to follow such a knight. "Give me your commands for I am your squire until the sun sets on eternity" They made a simple litter, using the two linen tunics, the wrestler's and Rhydian's, threaded through wooden staves, on which to carry the injured man over the rough road that led high into the mountains. Gathering all their belongings they bade the Inn Keeper farewell and set off into the darkening night, Rhydian walking beside the litter, pulled by a reluctant Cadair, Alain sitting on his back, with Cyfaill leading the way.

Walking nonstop throughout the night they reached the Abbey as the bell tolled for prime. One monk, seeing their plight, took them to the infirmary, uttering no words he indicated that they enter. The room was light and airy, with the scent of rosemary pervading the air, clear water bubbled from a spring, filling a stone trough in the dispensary. Laying his charge on a bed Rhydian spoke to the monk. "I believe this man was injured by my horse, I have travelled overnight to bring him into your care. His head wound I have cleaned, I ask you to set his leg, for this I cannot do, neither have I the skill in herbs to reduce his fever. I will be forever in your debt if you will help him."

Looking at the young man the monk broke silence. "My assistant is at the fair, I will need someone with strength and courage to help me in this work." Rhydian looked at the monk, then he replied "Give me but two hours to prepare myself and I will be your aide." Leaving Cadair's care to Alain Rhydian took the blanket from the wrestler, replacing it with another, then covering himself with Aldan's gift he found a place to sleep.

Dreams came quickly to him; colours swirled through space merging into shapes creating a landscape. Into this scene appeared nine maidens bathing in the water of a blue lake. They beckoned to the dreamer, enticing him to join them. At his approach two figures forsook the others, then, offering him food and drink they led him to the shore and sat him down on a bed of soft rushes, covering him in flowers.

The dark haired maiden spread her lace gown around her as she knelt beside the dreamer, with her fair haired companion on his other side. Two pairs of eyes, one of the deepest blue, the other as bright as the summer sky, opened wide with pleasure as they caressed his body, anointing him with salves, bringing comfort to his weary limbs. Then a mist rose up from the water, deepening until all vanished from sight.

Waking, after barely an hour's rest, yet feeling refreshed and with a sense of purpose, Rhydian returned to the wrestler's bedside where the monk had gathered his herbs and tools for the work ahead, for this he was untried and prayed for strength and courage in his task.

Chapter Twelve - Decisions to be made

In a quiet corner of the Abbey courtyard Rhydian sat alone, listening to the plain chant of Vespers, gathering his thoughts after the hard, long day. His mind went back to his sleep that morning, he could still feel the soothing hands of the two maids, unknown, but who were to him achingly familiar. His mind travelled even further back, to the demands of the long night's journey, when it seemed as if his charge would not be with them by daybreak.

He pondered on the reviving powers that had come from the stone cup, for it could be seen to make the pain easier to bear, keeping the fever at bay, yet it held only water, drawn from a mountain stream. He dwelt on the look of hate and loathing cast on him by the injured man, as if it would haunt him for all-time. He drew his blanket around him, once more gaining peace from the softly woven cloth, as if love itself was giving him protection from the world. Had the same magic driven the hate from his opponent's heart during the journey? Or did it choose whom it would serve?

His mind went forward to the day's happenings, the admiration he had for the skill and nerve of the healer had grown throughout the day. He felt a desire in himself to acquire the same knowledge, to have in his hands the ability to heal, to preserve life, not to lay claim to another's in combat. His mind was in conflict with the training he had received since childhood. He felt a shadow fall across him, as the Infirmerer, Brother Thomas, walked towards him, then stood quietly, looking down with a gentle concern. "May I join you here?" he asked "I believe you may be troubled and I would like to offer my help if you so desire"

Rhydian looked into the wise face of the monk, "You do indeed speak true, for now I doubt my chosen path, I would like to stay here, with you, in this newly endowed Abbey, to learn your skills, to spend my hours in quiet contemplation, exchanging thoughts with the brothers, for I find that I yearn to be a part of this community." Thomas replied gravely "I would dearly like to keep you, I know that soon my time will come, and if I can teach you well I would go happy that you will follow in my ways. But you have much to consider first, this life is a hard one, much of men's pleasures are denied to us, the love of a woman, the joy of seeing ones firstborn son, worldly treasures are not ours, you are as yet young and untried"

Rhydian raised his eyes, uncertainty and pain reaching out to the older man. "What must I do? How to choose which way to go, can I not remain here with you?" Thomas looked sternly back "Remember, you have promised your lord, the Prince Llywelyn, to travel to Castell y Bere. To join his retinue, a life you have not abhorred until now. I charge you to continue on your quest"

Then he rested his hand on Rhydian's shoulder, "Be not afraid, all will become clear to you soon, there are many routes that lead to the answer you seek, I will pray for you to receive guidance from a higher authority than me." At this he turned away. Rhydian reflected on all that had passed, then he made a decision, a way to see where his future should lie. He lay down under the starlit sky, his blanket wrapping him in a dreamless sleep that sweetly took away his fears and frets, finding his strength from deep within.

With the rising sun lighting the new day Rhydian searched for Alain, finding him in the stable, asleep on a soft bed of hay, horse and hound curled around the boy. He turned, leaving them still slumbering, he made his way towards the Infirmary with the low chant from Matins filling his mind. Brother Thomas greeted him, leading the way towards a low bed. "Our friend had a restful night; he tells me his name is Ythel, from Lys Kerwyd. He wishes to speak to you, I told him of your journey, he feels that he is beholden in this, it does not sit easy on a man such as him." The man stirred and looking at Rhydian he tried to speak, but his voice was so low Rhydian had to strain to catch his words.

"I had such hatred in my heart for you, I tried to steal your horse for my rewards, yet you brought me here, gave assistance to the good brother without any thought of gain. It is beyond my understanding" His brow was furrowed as he sought to find the reasons. Rhydian replied "Do not strive for answers, you needed help, this I gave, sleep now, when you wake I will be gone" Ythel spoke again, "Before you go I crave that you will talk with me once more, when I have regained my strength" Rhydian sighed, "So be it, I will return again before nightfall, now be at ease" Knowing that he must decide to leave the abbey, it would be hard to linger for his resolve may yet weaken, then together with Brother Thomas he went to the refectory. Where Alain eagerly greeted him, "I wondered whether Morpheus would have claimed you for all of today"

Rhydian smiled, gaining pleasure from his bright face. Cyfaill crept under his seat, resting her head on his knee; he could feel her body pressing tight against him. A rush of pure love ran through him for all that he held dear, could he leave these for a new path to take? He felt confused, he needed time alone, he would talk with Alain later, for now he drew breath and kept his thoughts and plans close.

Chapter Thirteen - Decisions Made

Early next morning, whilst it was still dark, Rhydian crept silently down to the stable to say goodbye to Cadair; Cyfaill, trying to follow, was turned back. "It will not be for long my friends, I am eager to leave before day breaks, look after Alain, I trust you" With that he picked up his pack and slipped quietly out of the Abbey grounds, then heading northwards he took the old track into the high mountains.

With birds greeting the new day, Rhydian joined the dawn chorus, letting his voice soar high on the wind, taking with it the tension of the long days past. The climb upwards was steep; Rhydian revelled in the hard walk, feeling his body working, numbing his mind. Reaching the top he stopped, looking backwards to the Abbey, half hidden by trees he could see the garden, visible as a patch of green among the grey stones. He sat down on the grass, enjoying the simple pleasure of silence, nothing to disturb him but the wind, birds and his own thoughts.

He recalled Ythel's words when they had talked late last night. There would be no more fights for him, but he had found peace within the abbey, and for as long as he desired, he was welcome to stay as a lay Brother. Rhydian had given the winnings acquired at the fair to Ythel, to pay for his keep until he could work. He knew that instead of an enemy, he had found a true friend, who valued the peace that now replaced the turmoil and the loneliness of his past life.

Before he remembered she was not there, Rhydian put out his hand, feeling for Cyfaill. His mind went to Alain, the burden of care placed on him rested heavy on his young shoulders, yet this was tempered by pride at the trust given to him. He would travel to the Mynach River, journeying alongside the abbey workmen, to the Devil's Bridge, there to wait for Rhydian to join him. In the warm sun and the peaceful quiet, Rhydian slept, the gentle breeze caressed him, no harm or troublesome thoughts disturbed him.

In his sleep he became a hawk who flew over land and sea, swooping down beside a lake, where, with an eye so keen and true he plucked a fish from the water, holding it in his sharp talons, settling on a stony crag to eat his feast. From this lofty perch he viewed the hills and moors, the beauty painted in wide brush stokes onto a natural canvas.

As he watched, the water stirred in the middle of the lake, creating a wave that flowed to the shore, there it crashed into foam, the water receding, revealing a woman, clad in a simple shift coloured with all the blues and greens of the skies and seas, head bowed, a gift from the water gods. A man came towards her, his arms outstretched in greeting, she enfolded him in her embrace as they stood in silence, so close, their hearts beating as one. The man looked upwards; the face of a young Emrys watched the Rhyd-Hawk, smiling as if he knew whose captive soul the dream bird carried. Slowly the pair began to walk into the water until they had disappeared from sight.

The hawk, gathering speed, flew northwards, until moving so fast all became a blur, nothing could impede the heedless flight. As he slowed down, a headland spread out below him, jutting out into the sea. Over the blue water a small boat plied its way across a narrow rocky passage, sailing towards an island. It carried three women, who wept over the still form of a man. Steering the boat was a man with long grey hair and a flowing beard, whilst waiting ashore for them stood a group of monks, with a litter made ready to receive the wounded man and convey him to the island monastery. Stepping out of the boat, the old man looked up at the sky and Emrys smiled and saluted the circling hawk. With a sudden start Rhydian awoke, still in a dreamlike trance, he gathered his wits, the feel of the wind on his face, and the thrill of the flight remaining deep within him. Once more taking the hidden pathways over the mountains, he wondered about the Dream-Hawk and the Fayes, who inhabited those watery places.

Rhydian looked at the hard terrain he had to traverse. Deep valleys cut into the hillsides with the high plain windswept and bare; here was no shelter to be found. No habitation to seek refuge in on stormy nights, lonely, with nature asking questions of the traveller. Had he the physical power required, as well as the inner strength needed? He cleared his mind of all the petty debris that could hinder the thinking that he so much needed, then, with one last backwards glance, he strode out. Keeping the sun to his right, he went, straight as a lance, over the beautiful, forbidding hills. He found water, fast running, clear and cool, he took shelter in sparse valley meadows, with sheep, deer and the wild black cattle grazing beside him. His thoughts chased around his head, creating a never ending circle of doubts to be faced before any decisions could be made. In the quiet, music came unbidden to him, songs of love, hymns of praise. Emotions, often hidden inside, took hold and drowned him with their power. At night sleep came easily, renewing him by daybreak, when the sun's light woke him, returning him to his thoughts again.

Soon his journey's end was close, he could see the river far below, now was the time for him to choose between the abbey and contentment, or the world and all the heartache it brings. The time alone had been welcome, now he knew the way to take. Standing by the bridge that spanned the treacherous river, a boy and hound kept watch, as they did every day. The dog suddenly sprang with a bound, giving tongue, she ran up the narrow path, the boy followed, hope rising. In the distance, arms outstretched ran another boy, his voice calling them, he knelt down as the hound reached him, and with eyes, bright with tears, he waited for his young friend. Gone forever his doubts and fears, he knew now where his future lay.

Chapter Fourteen - Alain's Tale

Crossing the narrow bridge that spanned the river Rhydian was filled with admiration for the plucky men who had built it across the high narrow gorge of the Mynach, where ferns grew from the rocky walls, drenched by water cascading down the falls. In the stable yard close by, Cadair, hearing a beloved voice, whinnied loudly, restless until he felt a hand running along his side, an arm on his neck, pressed into his warm coat, Rhydian, full with tears of love welling up inside his heart. *"I will not leave you again that is my promise, we will all face the world together"*

Rhydian slept well that night, no dreams or visions came to disturb him; he woke refreshed, ready for the next part of his journey. This was a hard route to traverse, over wild mountains where wolves may yet be found, with the need to travel swiftly and safely over the adverse terrain. Alain, to his delight, now rode his own horse, a sturdy cob, nimble, well used to the mountain paths. They kept to the river's edge, climbing steadily passing lonely farmsteads, where smoke rose from the hearths, until they reached the lowest slopes of the hills, here with shelter, lush grazing and game to hunt, they made their camp, baking freshly caught trout in the ashes of their fire. As the flames grew dormant Alain began to talk, hesitantly at first, as if afraid to open his deepest thoughts.

"I have often caught the wild ponies at home, then ridden them 'til being thrown, but never before has such a gift been bought for me. I will cherish her forever, I shall call her Bronn, after my father - and my brother" Alain tried to stem a tear, and remained silent

55

for a while, then in a low voice he continued "As a child I would hide when my mother was sad, as she often was, she would sit for long hours gazing into the river by our home, my sister would care for me, though but a child herself. We would have days of freedom, where we could roam the hills unhindered. Then one day all that ceased, Mam kept us close by, afraid lest we strayed out of her calling.

Gwendydd, my sister, told me stories as I grew older, how our father had taken Bron with him on a journey, following the Prince Madoc to distant lands. Mam begged him not to take Bron, but to no avail. They shared the gift I lack, that of seeing each other when by water, she could watch him and know all was well. She knew they would not come back, that my father died, and so Bron grew to manhood on distant shores, then one day she saw him no more.

That was when our carefree hours finished for a time, until one day, sitting by the river, looking as always deep into the water, Gwen saw among strange animals, a young boy, with bare, dark skin. She called to Mam, and the two stared, quite intent for a while, looking into the water, then with a long sigh Mam went indoors. From that day she was more content to let us wander, as long as we stayed together, but Gwen was sent away, to my Lord Llywelyn's castle, to be taught the ways of a lady. I could no longer go alone, for she knew, I had not the sight."

Alain paused for breath. "I thought it strange when told, ere you arrived, that I would soon be travelling with a knight. Mam was watching for your arrival, she knew who you were, what you looked like, and that I would be safe with you. She warned me to be heedful of strangers, to give you support and take note of your chivalry. I believe that you also have the sight, not yet, methinks, as keen as Mam's or Gwen's, but sufficient for others to watch over you, I give thanks for now I've met you, and my future and my life have changed forever."

The next day, as they climbed higher the land around seemed familiar to Rhydian, yet he had not travelled here before. He turned eastwards to the highest point, eyes seeking the spot where the dream Rhyd-Hawk had perched. "I know that there is a lake up there, I must go to see it." Cadair, feeling his excitement broke into a canter, leaving a cloud of dust for Alain and Cyfaill to follow. At the top he stopped, gazing down at the dark, cool water of the cwm. The sun's rays reflected flashes of pure gold dancing over the pool as if it was on fire. Slowly, he rode down to the water's edge, there dismounting, he waited. From a distance Alain kept watch and wondered, not understanding what disturbed his friend, but patiently holding back his questions until the time was right. After some while Rhydian spoke.

"Can your sister Gwen summon your Mam to speak to her, or must they just bide by the water and wait?" Alain replied "I know that if Bron was in danger or sad, Mam could sense it, she would sit and wait after he had gone, often all day, until she saw him, they did not speak. She said that Gwen had more strength than her and could command her from long distances, but I have no power at all." He seemed saddened by his lack of sight, as if it made him a lesser person.

"Emrys would tell me about his own sister, called Gwendydd too, that there was none stronger than her. She could be in one place and when sleeping, would appear elsewhere. Sometimes I think our Gwen can also do this." Rhydian considered this, and then asked a question "Alain, who is Emrys? I have seen him here, in a dream, you know him well, tell me more"

"My grandmother died when Mam was a day old, Emrys came and took her to live with him. We call him our Taid, but if he is I cannot say. He does not age, being always a very old man." Rhydian was thoughtful, then with one last look at the lake he remounted going northwards, as he had flown when the dream Rhyd-Hawk.

Chapter Fifteen - The Fight

The weather was kind to the travellers; the nights were warm and days of glorious sunshine in which to enjoy the peace and beauty of the place. They tarried by streams, talked long into the night, telling tales of knights and adventure. Slowly they crossed the land of five peaks whose heights gave birth to five rivers flowing freely to the seas in their own joyful dance.

During this time Rhydian taught Alain how to fight with the sword and using a straight young sapling, created a lance. Taking his knightly accoutrements out of their coverings he showed him how to dress himself and Cadair, as a squire should. The big destrier did not allow anyone other than those he trusted to place the gaudy trappings on his back, but Alain had already gained his love and he stood, in quietness, whilst the young boy struggled with the heavy caparison. Rhydian carried no shield or mail, for these remained at Castell Du. Just his sword and its tooled scabbard, shining brightly with Alain's proud care.

The path over the high peaks led steeply to the river Dyfi, where small hamlets lay along the river as it meandered through meadows until reaching the open seas. Steadily descending they reached shelter among the trees, with welcome grazing and more game to follow than on higher ground. Rhydian gently caressed Cyfaill in the warming glow of the firelight.

"Methinks you eat too well, you get fat!" Alain laughed, "For such a clever knight you know very little! Your hound bitch is pregnant, not fat" Rhydian was shocked and concerned. "I must not take her over such rough ground; she needs to be cared for." Alain

59

asked who the stud dog was. Rhydian looked blank, for his father bred but carefully, no dog from home had sired these pups, yet what other? An image came to mind, that of Cyfaill at play with the large wolfhound of Emrys'. He looked in awe at her as she lay asleep so peacefully. "Rhydian, you must not fuss her now, she is fit and strong and there is a long while yet before she whelps"

That night he slept fitfully, uneasy, he took his sword and laid one hand on its flat blade, the other held the hilt, for he felt they were being watched by unfriendly eyes. The fire died down, the moon was hidden by clouds, so shapes could barely be seen. The hound's sharp nose and eyes alerted Rhydian to figures moving towards the camp, but before he could awaken Alain, they attacked. His long training from lords of battle made him react quickly, Cyfaill kept one at bay, another held Alain down, while a third circled Rhydian, with a large stave clasped in his hands. His face was brown from many years under the sun; his clothes were ragged and coarse. For a moment he felt a shaft of fear run through him, then anger broke through, these two powerful forces created a potent mixture, and with a loud roar Sir Rhydian fought with all the skill he had learned.

In truth, it did not last long; Cadair came to Alain's aid and Cyfaill's quarry turned quickly, running off. Rhydian knocked the man to the ground, cutting the stave in two; he lifted his sword up high, ready to strike. Slowly he lowered his arm, for he found at the point of victory, he could not take another's life. The defeated man lay still not daring to move, gripped with fear, waiting for this young knight to kill.

Rhydian quietly took him by the hand and lifted him up. "Go in peace friend and learn all is not what it may seem" Then he watched the man as he rejoined the others in the shelter of the trees. Alain looked at him strangely, uncertain what to say. "Why did you let him go? He would have killed us if they had been the victors" Rhydian answered with a rueful smile "I know not, I have been taught to fight, but not to kill, and when I faced reality I failed. In truth, I felt it was not right, but was this my conscience or my fear?"

He did not sleep again that night but strummed his crwth singing quietly to himself. The music ran around Alain's head, soothing him, inducing the sleep that eluded his friend. The events of the night caused Rhydian much soul searching, were they portents for the future? Could he be a true Knight if he failed in the last act? Although he did not regret his action yet he could not deny its impact.

He longed to talk to someone to help him wrestle this demon. He thought of Emrys, or Thomas, he desired so much the wisdom of his father, who had known battles yet still desired peace. He wrapped himself in Aldan's blanket, with its welcome release from stress and gathered his thoughts.

As dawn broke they continued towards the river, avoiding all houses, taking the road to the old fort, crossing fords over the winding rivers. Rhydian shut his mind to all visions of water sprites, afraid they would weaken his resolve to travel fast. He must forgo his delights and follow his liege Lord's directions; already the journey had taken too long. From the fort he took the direct route over the ridges of high land. A strong wind blew in from the sea, heavily laden with salt leaving a rich taste on his tongue, he very much wanted to go to the shores, but was in haste, so he turned his back and rode onward, reaching the far side by nightfall.

Castell y Bere sat on top of a hill, with its partly built walls marking out the extent of the new Castle, Rhydian was suddenly fearful. His journey had been an adventure, but now that he had arrived, found he did not want to stay, desiring instead to seek the answer to many questions. There were paths for him to follow, to explore. A blue eyed water sprite who beckoned, showing visions and dreams to unravel. Could he exchange all of that for a life at court, with trivial pastimes and mock fights to pass the time in unreal strife?

He waited quietly for Alain to prepare Cadair, donned his tabard, and strapped his sword to his side, once ready the party rode through the gate as Rhydian led them to meet the Prince Llywelyn.

Part Three

The
Court

Chapter Sixteen - The Prince's Court

Prince Llywelyn's new Castle stood on a small hill with the flood plains of two rivers creating a natural moat on three sides, the fourth side protected by the mountain, rising steeply upwards. The half built stone walls of the unfinished tower keep formed a black silhouette against the red sky of sunset, its edges burnished gold by the dying rays. Passing through opened gates, they reached a courtyard overflowing with people and animals. Rhydian dismounted, with Alain left on guard he entered the hall, where at a great table, laden with food and drink, sat the prince by whose command Rhydian's journey began. Had it been a trivial bidding, long since forgotten in his busy days, or a measured charge, seeking to guide a man along his allotted path?

The young knight stood tall as he spoke to his liege lord, "If it may please you sire, I have done your bidding and await your orders" for a moment there was silence, then Llywelyn rose and walked towards him, laughing with pleasure, "Your absence has been noted. Daily I have been asked when you will arrive" Rhydian looked puzzled, for who was there here that knew, or cared, about him? With a smile Llywelyn beckoned to a chair beside his "Come, sit by me, keep me enthralled with your adventures, I am bored with old tales and need something new to lighten the long evenings"

Rhydian inclined his head, then spoke "Firstly I must request directions to stabling for my horses, then lodgings for my companion, they are tired and in need of sustenance, I cannot rest myself, until they are properly cared for" At this reply the prince smiled, "As my guest you may keep your horses with mine, your companion is welcome here, to join with me" he turned to a young man standing behind him, "Tegwared give our friend assistance, and I foresee on his return, a night of entertainment"

Tegwared led them to the castle stables watching as Rhydian settled both horses and hound for the night, fetching fresh hay and straw, pouring cool water into the trough, he found this strange and asked why a knight worked thus, for surely that was the squire's duty.

Rhydian laughed, but made no response, then, all done, they returned to the lofty hall. Llywelyn beckoned to seats along the dais, pushing a trencher, full of meat and bread, towards them. Taking a flagon of deep red, heady wine, he filled a goblet and handed it to Rhydian, which he quietly set aside, taking instead a flagon of water. As the prince had ordered he began to relate his journey, a fine tale, told without falter.

Yet he found a reluctance to tell the whole, no mention was made of the water sprite with her dark hair and deep, deep, blue eyes. Nor were his dreams told, afraid they might be misunderstood. As his tale came to an end some were ready for sleep, others, head fuelled by wine were seeking a new sport, looking for a woman to warm their bed. They left the hall, promising to return soon with a lusty wench for Rhydian. He turned quite pale, and stood up to leave, begging indulgence from his Lord, saying he yearned for rest after his long day. With a curious stare Prince Llywelyn bid him goodnight. Together with Alain, Rhydian went to the place where he felt safe, sleeping until the daylight, shining through the stable door, woke them.

The castle was quiet, apart from the villeins, no one was yet astir so early in the morning as Rhydian rode Cadair out. Going fast through lanes and meadows he reached the river. Stripping off his clothes he ran into the water, the cold making him draw sharp breaths. He chased silver fish, diving down to the reeds, a bold otter swam with him, proving to be a better hunter by catching his breakfast, which he ate whilst lying on his back, his bright beady eye watching warily, ever ready to take flight.

Climbing out onto the bank Rhydian reached for his clothes, blindly brushing the water from his face, he felt a shadow fall across him. Looking up he saw a face, softer in the morning light than when reflected through the river. Without feeling shame in his nakedness he reached out and touched her face for the first time, creating a flame that coursed through his body, waking senses that had, until now, lain dormant.

With sudden awareness of time and place he hastily donned his clothes, the potent presence of this young maiden causing him some confusion. Together they rode back, her arms encircling his waist, her cheek resting on his shoulder, her long black hair lying across his face. As they reached the stable Alain ran out, in sheer delight, calling loudly "Rhydian, Gwendydd". His joy was without bounds at the sight of his two most beloved people, together.

Chapter Seventeen - The Challenge

From the dark shadows of the castle walls a still figure watched as Gwen embraced her young brother, noting every move she made, how her waist was encircled by the young knight's arm, with her head resting on his shoulder. As the sound of her voice, with its lilting cadence, reached the onlooker, words drowned by the everyday noises from the castle, his thoughts grew blacker and hatred grew for the newcomer. The girl suddenly moved, as if aware of time passing, she fled back to the lady tower. Keeping out of sight, the silent watcher followed her, entering the main hall to rejoin the Prince's retinue, there he awaited the return of Rhydian.

When he entered later, Llywelyn greeted him with laughter, "Sir Rhydian, you are an early riser, I see we will have to give up our feasting if we wish to catch you. Sit here, by the fire with me; you intrigue me, not being in the usual fashion of a young man. Last night I saw your dislike of our rowdy melee, you left the hall suddenly, in full flight, yet you do not have the look of a monk"

With a wry smile Rhydian replied "Sometimes I prefer quieter pastimes, yet am not, I trust, a killjoy. I can tell tales, sing and play songs, with rhymes as bawdy as the rest, but I also like to keep my own company, with time for much thought. It is true I withdrew from the lusty games, but I vowed to refrain from Venus' sport until my quest is done, I entreat you not to divert me along my chosen pathway."

The prince, gazing at the upright figure, felt a moment of sadness for the day when he too, had held such high ideals. "I will not stand in your way, but trust that whilst you remain here with me there will be time, before your quest, whatever that may be, takes you further, gracing us with your company, fighting in our tourneys, breaking a few maidens hearts along the way, and then singing us to sleep when our bodies are tired"

Smiling with pleasure at this command Rhydian turned to Tegwared. "Will you also be at the jousts? There will be much demand for places I am sure" A strange look passed over the face of the prince's son, and his voice had a sharp ring to it as he replied –"I look forward to a bout against you, but I must give you fair warning the tilt is my favourite sport, in which I am unbeaten" Tegwared threw his gauntlet down on the floor, "A challenge match to whet the appetite. You do not yet know, but we have a score to settle, better to be soon and not delay."

Quietly Rhydian picked up the gauntlet "I accept, but have the right to know why you have challenged me, you need not fret, I will meet you, but I do not fight without reason" The answer came in tones so low only the two could hear it, "The Lady Gwen is my betrothed, I will land the fatal blow that will lay waste your pathetic hopes"

No word had passed between them since the challenge, with the gauntlet thrown down; Rhydian watched as Tegwared led a hunting party that departed from the castle grounds, seeking game to replenish the larders, leaving a confused and sorrowful young man behind, feeling lost and alone in this strange place. Turning towards the stable he looked up at the ramparts, to the lady tower, in his imagination seeing the slim figure of Gwen, wishing his hearts desire was beside him now. He reflected that if she was truly betrothed, he must abide by the Knight's code of conduct, either claiming her through battle or to forever relinquish his rights.

As he brushed Cadair, the steady rhythmic physical action calmed his heated mind. From the doorway he heard a quiet voice speaking softly to him, words that reached deep into his very soul. With a sharp intake of breath he took her in his arms, tears running freely down his cheeks, he buried his face in her hair. With all the gentleness of a mother, not fully understanding his pain, she soothed it away until he regained full command of his senses.

With her arms around him they sat on sweet smelling hay, Cyfaill's head resting on Gwen's kirtle. Rhydian retold the day's encounter with Tegwared, fearful of her reply. As he spoke anger rose in her, until she could not contain it, there was an edge to her voice as she replied "I revoke that, I am not his betrothed, never have been nor ever will be. He has lusted after me since I first arrived; he often comes, unbidden, to the solar room, thinking that, as the Prince is his father, all will fall at his feet. The Princess Joan will have no truck with him. His noble sire views him kindly, favouring him highly above others; luck seems to flow in his blood. He has a ready wit, good looks and is an accomplished knight, but I cannot like him, he can be cruel, in ways I do not care for, I tread very carefully in my dealings with him."

After a few minutes of silence they talked again. Gwen telling how she had often watched Rhydian as a boy, in visits to his home by the power of her sight, seeing him at play, how sad she was when he left home and her happiness when he returned. "I noted your care for the frail and how deft you were with sick creatures; you were not like the others, never wantonly unkind. I have loved you well for most of my life, you are the other half of my soul, I find that without you I am nothing, an empty vessel, with no guiding star to follow."

For a long while they talked in the peace of the stable forgetting what the morrow might bring, until Alain found them with the orders to return, one to her duties, the other to entertain his liege's court. Their idyll past for now, with more stories yet to be told, they obeyed the summons.

Early on the next morning Rhydian spoke to the Prince, professing his love for Gwen and hers for him. The full story he did not tell, nor was it asked of him, in the hours they spent in each other's company a respect grew between the hardened leader of men and the idealistic youth. "Rest easy, I will speak to my ardent son, in my court no maid should fear for her honour, nor to be forced into unwelcome alliances. The Lady Gwen, as my ward, has my protection and due regard should be given to her wishes." With a lightened spirit Rhydian sought his beloved, finding her with the ladies attending to the Princess Joan. A taut look crossed Gwen's face as she saw him leaving the great hall, turning to joy as he smiled at her. He spoke boldly to the company, "You see here a boy, his heart pierced by cupids arrows, who craves of you a short time, a few moments with the Lady Gwendydd"

Amid much laughter the ladies withdrew from the room, leaving the two young lovers alone. There, sitting inside the private chapel they plighted their troth. Rhydian, taking Emrys' ring, threaded it onto a leather thong, to wear around her neck. "I cannot promise you any riches, for the road that I tread may be rough, I am going I know not where. But I know without you I dread the days ahead. You are my mirrored half, yet I do not ask you to face these dangers with me, only to be my haven when I am in need. If it should please you to share my journey we will walk together, equal partners in all we do" Holding Emrys' ring in her hands, feeling its warmth, she replied "If you are by my side, I am afraid of nothing"

As he kissed her the door opened wide and Alain rushed in, unable to contain his pleasure, "I could no longer bide my time and wait, you have been ages" Gwen laughed, saying "You take not just me, but my little brother as well, heed well this fair warning, for I almost forgot that he will give us no peace, wanting forever to be part of our adventures" Rhydian put both his arms around the pair "Remember you must also take my horse and hound – and her pups, soon to arrive!!!"

With this they returned to the hall their happiness visible to all who saw them. But so quickly hope can give way to fear, as the sound of hooves clattering over the cobbled yard heralding the return of the hunting party. Tegwared halted his sweating mount in front of Rhydian. Then, without a word, he turned away.

Chapter Eighteen - The Tourney

Gwen returned, troubled, to her bower, watching as Rhydian slowly made his way to the hall where Tegwared and his cronies, still full of the chase, were holding sway. At his entrance the voices became quiet all eyes were upon him, waiting for events to unfold. Holding a straight course past the party Rhydian walked up to the Prince, taking a seat next to him at the high table amidst much welcome. The talk soon came round to the tourney, Llywelyn and his sons led their own teams whose valour and fame were legend across the kingdoms. "A place must be found for you" The hint of a smile touched his lips. "I believe you would be happier in my team than my son's. The trial of strength between us is not taken lightly so practice hard to ensure I do not lose"

The favour shown Rhydian by the Prince was well marked, causing some to choose him as a friend, others to harbour ill will and resentment against this newcomer. Rhydian kept his distance from all others, preferring his own company, with the summer evenings bringing untold joy with Gwen. An older knight, Sir Bedwyn, befriended him, giving advice in the rules of jousting; he also brought with him news of Tegwared, whose venomous tongue had spread unfounded tales, creating a figure of hate. The day of the tourney dawned amid much bustle and excitement, with late arrivals camping outside the castle walls.

For the first time since he was knighted, Rhydian wore his regalia, with its specially designed blazon, donned over borrowed armour. Whilst Alain prepared Cadair, Rhydian knelt in front of his sword and prayed silently for courage, for he knew that he faced an opponent who abhorred him, and would seek to bring humiliation to the man who had thwarted his desire for the Lady Gwendydd.

Llywelyn had set the rules of combat, which would require a steady hand, clear head and brave heart. The melee a pied was drawing to its close as Rhydian left the stable, seeking the tree where his shield hung. Fear suddenly rose inside him; he began to shake, to doubt himself. He scanned the crowds his eyes searching amongst the people, seeking for a familiar face; then he saw him, the wise old man of his dreams, Emrys. It seemed as if time stood still, no sound was heard except inside his head, the sound of a crwth playing such sweet music. Without a word passing between them, his courage returned.

Before mounting Cadair he spoke gently to him "We have had many adventures, much sport together now I place my trust in you, carry me boldly, without fear, be sure footed and steadfast, together we will be the victors." He led him to the nearby block, and with Alain's help mounted him, eager to start the fray, he rode onto the field with his lance held high.

The Heralds called for the knights to make ready then, with a mighty cry, the two great horses thundered towards each other. The lances aims were true and each found its target. Turning the horses around the knights came back for the second tilt. Once more the match was even, yet it seemed as if Tegwared's anger was rising, for in this favourite sport, he was deemed to be the champion. The third and final run began; the heavy lance unbalancing the lighter Rhydian, Tegwared struck him full on his shield, Rhydian, keeping a straight arm, also made hard contact. Cadair did not waver, enabling his rider to stay upright. Tired, Tegwared's horse stumbled, and with no time to recover the Prince's son tumbled to the ground.

In fury he unsheathed his sword and ran to Rhydian. "We have not finished, I have the right of combat, fight me like a man hand to hand" With his blade he slashed out wildly, cutting Cadair's leg 'til it bled, Rhydian throwing off his helm, dismounted. The two fought savagely, their feet slid on the trampled grass as they forgot the joust, that this was but a game. With the blood pounding in both their veins they battled on, trying to maim the other in defeat. One went down, the other closed in for the final thrust. Their eyes met, death facing the loser, the sword descended hard, with dust rising, as it fell harmlessly to the ground.

Rhydian turned and with scalding tears flowing down his cheeks walked back to Cadair, not hearing the crowd's jeers, branding him a coward at the final point.

Chapter Nineteen - The Aftermath

In the quiet coolness of the stable as he tended to Cadair's injured fetlock, Rhydian gathered his troubled thoughts. Feeling a deep shame he tried to block the jeers of the crowd from his mind. He saw again the strickened look on the face of his opponent as he lay on the floor, remembered how all anger had left him, leaving in its place the desire to weep at the stupidity of man.

A low voice called, full of love and pride, before turning to meet her, Rhydian drew himself up straight, yet unable to hide his greatest fear, that of rejection from those he cared for most. Gwen moved towards him, taking him in her arms they stood together in silence, soothed by the closeness of their warm bodies, with no need for words to pass between them. Into this peace came the old knight Bedwyn, "This should have been foreseen I saw you had the gift of grace in your soul. Be not shamed, you are still a true warrior, yet forged from a different metal to others here. My Lord Llywelyn sent me here as courier, bidding me to bring you to him, he desires to speak with you"

"I cannot leave my destrier untended, tell my lord I will come when my squire returns" Giving this reply Rhydian returned to the care of his horse. The older man, sitting down in the straw, looked at the young man with respect for his unique form of bravery, to put an animal before the ruler of the land, to risk his wrath. "I will wait here, with you and your lady; it is many years since I have met your equal"

The door burst open, causing to Gwen to cry with alarm as Alain struggled in, carrying Cyfaill in his arms; he was covered in blood, sweat ran from his brow as he placed her on the ground. He gently wiped the mud from her body as she took deep breaths between whimpers of pain. Words tumbled out of his mouth, between great gasps of breath "She came to my aid when I was fighting Tegwared's friends, I am sorry, I must take the blame, they kicked her, then ran away, laughing at the pain inflicted. She could not stand, so I carried her back here"

Rhydian knelt by the hound, her tongue licked his hand as he talked softly to her, stroking her body gently. "I believe she will whelp within the hour, brought on too early by the blows received, she needs help, but I have no knowledge of these matters" The anguish in his voice brought Bedwyn to his side. "She will be well, being young and strong, but not so the pups lying within. We must keep them warm and dry when they are born, mayhap they will not draw breath without our aid, I will show you what to do if needed, she just needs more time, and your presence will be her comfort and reassurance. Rhydian took Emrys stone cup, which he filled with water, giving it to Cyfaill to drink; as her breathing grew quieter she drifted into a peaceful, healing sleep. Inside the stable it was still, only the sound of breathing could be heard, as all within slept.

The hound began to stir, waking the young knight who lay beside her. Slowly he crept to Bedwyn, asking for advice and guidance. They watched over Cyfaill as she struggled to give birth, a large head black began to appear first, then a wet body emerged. Taking a large handful of straw Bedwyn began to rub the lifeless pup, blowing gently into its nose, suddenly it sneezed and taking a breath began whimpering. Trembling with excitement Rhydian laid it beside Cyfaill. Gwen and Alain, now awake, danced with joy as yet another pup began to arrive. But there was also heart ache as one small body did not draw breath.

The door opened and a tall figure entered unnoticed. At first he was angry, but this soon changed as looking on, he observed the small group, so intent in their work. Alain was the first to see him, in surprise his tiny charge nearly slipped from his hands. The Prince taking it from him hushed the cries, then placed it down on the straw bed beside Cyfaill, who for one last time tried to deliver her biggest pup. Seeming to lack the strength for this final effort, she started to shiver. The tears in Rhydian's eyes blocked out the face of the large man who knelt down beside him, All he knew was that a pair of knowing hands gently eased the trapped limb and with a rush the last of the litter arrived.

It was a few minutes before the realization of who their visitor was dawned on Rhydian. He stood before Llywelyn with a sensation of deep foreboding, for ignoring a summons was serious, yet felt no need to explain his lack of attention. There before him Llywelyn saw bravery such as made Saints, but that track would not be journeyed down by this youth.

Time stood still as man and boy took measure of each other until Llywelyn began to laugh, "By my troth, I take the greatest pleasure in being taught a lesson in humility by my youngest knight, who reminds me that a lowly hound is as important in the eyes of our Lord as I am. Gwen, I do not believe he is so holy that I can leave you here with him all night, return to my lady wife, Sir Rhydian you will be at the Hall in the morning, do not fail me this time, twice would be too many, until then I bid you farewell, come Gwendydd"

Without a backward glance he left, followed by Gwen and Bedwyn, leaving Rhydian and Alain with their thoughts, for the morn may not bode well if Tegwared should speak first to his sire.

Chapter Twenty – Dismissal

All night long Rhydian kept vigil over Cyfaill and her litter. Four pups she nursed, one small body sadly buried under an oak tree in the pleasance. He had found great peace in watching the new lives as they sought to find their place. Later, walking towards the hall, he wondered what the future would bring. A knight's life may not be the path for him to travel, sure in the knowledge that his lord had no need for one who failed to carry through the final blows. He remembered the troubled look his mother had given him as she gave him her farewell kiss and blessing, had she known her son would be unable to take another man's life?

The hall was empty except for the Prince seated at the high table, as Rhydian approached. "Have no fears, I wish to relate an old tale about a man and his dog, how the man had acted in haste, not looking for the truth first." He beckoned to a seat beside him, then continued. "Many years ago, a hunter laid his baby son in its cot, leaving his hound to guard him from the wolves still roaming the hills. On his return he found the dog, with its mouth foaming and bloody. The baby's cradle was empty, believing the hound had harmed his son, he killed the dog without a thought. A sound from behind the settle led him to find the truth; his young son lay unharmed beside the body of a wolf. Had that man learnt to stay his anger and reflect, then a noble life would not have been taken." He paused for a moment, then gathering his thoughts spoke again.

"Sir Rhydian, I was that man. Do not believe that I have forsaken you when I say you must leave my court, but others here have yet to grow in understanding, putting your life in peril. I am beset by people of little vision, who will not see in you the courage it takes to be different in thought and deed. You have a lineage to be proud of – a father of integrity, a mother whose compassion is greatly known – yet you cannot remain with me, I must harden my heart – much though I desire that you remain here at court. I have kept the peace in my lands for many long years, hard fought by a show of strength; your ways would cause my enemies to ask questions about my leadership. The time will come when my task is done, but not yet, my sons have not learnt the skills they require. You must leave before Tegwared awakes."

Rhydian replied "Sire, I will leave in my own time I shall not flee like a thief in the night" Llywelyn responded with understanding "If not for yourself, for Gwen, I cannot keep her ever in my sight, she will not be safe if you stay here to remind my vengeful son of his humiliation." Rhydian considered this, "I must be certain of my way, with but an hour's grace, you will have my answer" Llywelyn could only nod his assent, the sorrow he felt was greater than he could bear, watching the man he would have been proud to call son walk away from him, to face the world, unbowed.

Leaving the hall Rhydian found Gwen waiting for him, eager to hear his news. In measured tones he told how he had but an hour to decide if he would do as the Prince commanded. Fear turned Gwen cold at the thought of losing him; he was her life blood without which she would surely die. He knew time was short before Tegwared awoke, but Gwen smiled "He will sleep late today, the sun had begun its climb in the sky before he retired to bed, and the Lady Joan slipped a draught in his wine last night, no love is lost between those two, and she has a weakness for me."

Gwen picked up a bundle neatly wrapped and tossed it in a corner "I have the few belongings that I desire to take from here, I have money too for our journey. When we plighted our troth you said we would find our pathway together, I keep my word, you will see I am my mother's daughter!" As a great weight lifted from Rhydian's shoulders excitement began to grow inside him, he began to plan their leaving, suddenly the joy left him. "I cannot leave Cyfaill behind, yet how can I take her too?" Laughing, Gwen took him inside the saddle room, pointing to two woven panniers. "Bronn is strong, she can easily carry our belongings, Alain and Cyfaill's pups, Cadair will willingly carry us"

Rhydian gave his lady a long hard look of admiration; he may have the dreams, but the power to take them through to reality was hers." I will ask Alain if he wishes to come with us, or stay here and make his future at Llywelyn's court, where he would be well received." Whilst Gwen returned to the Lady Joan Rhydian sought out Alain, finding him curled up asleep next to Cyfaill, her head on his lap and the tiny roan bitch pup nestling in his hand. When Rhydian asked the question Alain grew angry, "What manner of man do you think I am? I would lay down my life to save yours. You insult me by even thinking I could remain here"

These words brought colour to Rhydian's face. "Forgive me, I did not intend to hurt you, but no one should travel with me except of their own free will. I will be honoured for you to join us. Gwen had begun to plan our going last night, before I knew the need was there, she is a wise woman." Alain gave a shout of laughter, "Be warned, she will cozen you with soft words, but rule you with an iron fist, be in no doubt, for I suffered much when she had me in her charge" Rhydian gently ran his hand down Cadair's leg, feeling for heat, aware that there was no time for the wound to heal. Alain started to make ready for their leaving whilst Rhydian sought out Llywelyn in the Castle keep to bid him farewell.

The Prince looked at the young man, "You have much that I envy, loyal friends, a lady worthy of your love and a pure spirit as yet untarnished. Were I younger, without my royal duties, I would have liked to join you in your quest. But I have chosen my path, bringing its own reward, I trust my name will be remembered for many years after I have left this mortal world" Taking his sword he kissed the hilt, then, with a sigh, he dismissed Rhydian.

No-one watched as their party left the Castell, except for two old men. Bedwyn stood waiting by the gate for them to pass through, "Godspeed, I have kept guard, the young knights are still sleeping soundly, you will be long gone when they wake. I do not say goodbye, but farewell for I know that we will meet at least one more time." Then he looked across the valley to where another pair of keen old eyes was watching the strangely touching group as they started another step of the journey. The big horse proudly bore his Lady, whilst the steady Bronn carefully carried the mother and her pups, bound to each other by their friendship.

Part Four

The
Quest

Chapter Twenty One - Cadair Idris

Climbing steadily they left the castle far below, not stopping until a fair distance lay between them and Tegwared. The three peaks of Cadair Idris rising above, beckoning them to unseen places, with the promise of new adventures along the way. Their companionable silence was broken only by the wind blowing over the grass, the birds signalling their presence in song and by the puppies' occasional cries as they lay warm and snug in the large panniers slung across Bronn's broad back. Their pace was slower than Rhydian wanted, but fears for Cadair's wound and with Cyfaill not yet recovered from her whelping, he was forced to curb his desire to reach the safety of high ground.

Stopping by a stream that coursed its way down the valley, with good grazing and shelter from the mountains stony walls, they made camp. Later, sitting by the fire, Rhydian began to speak "The mountain calls to me, I once had a dream which I now must follow. Alain, I trust you to care for my lady until I return" Gwen looked troubled as he spoke "You intend to spend the night alone on the chilly mountain? Men have lost their wits after a night on Cadair Idris"

Rhydian smiled at her, "A vigil you may keep, watch out for me by a blue lake, where I saw, through the eyes of a hawk, a damsel walk into its water with a man. I will await their return, I have great need of speech with them" Gwen watched him run swiftly up the steep track through eyes drenched with tears, unable to stem them as they ran freely down her cold cheeks, until he disappeared from sight. With a deep sigh she went to the stream and by taking large stones created a small pool of clear water, then sitting by its edge and in the way of women across the centuries, she waited.

The sun had just dropped behind the mountain as Rhydian reached the lake, casting long shadows across the surface, changing its colours to green and black, from blue and gold. Suddenly a wind sprang up, forming white waves that danced to the shores edge. Music started to play, reverberating around the mountain sides, growing louder until it roared with intensity. All around rocks began to change shape, mythical creatures let loose from captivity. Rhydian concentrated his mind, bringing sweet thoughts to banish his fear, with Gwen's lovely face held in his heart he walked calmly towards the lake.

The waves parted, revealing a path that led downwards to a cave, where stood a slender figure beckoning Rhydian to enter. He hesitated, fearing to descend into the watery realm, then, with courage returned, he followed her through the cave's portal. Here light was soft, music gentle, a feeling of peace surrounded him, time ceased, and he felt immortal. As his eyes began to close, an unnatural sleep tried to claim him, through the air he could hear a voice calling to him, urgent, growing louder bringing him back from the brink of surrendering himself to this otherworld.

He looked in wonder at the kingdom under the lake, peopled by maidens of beauty such as he had never seen before. Singing that almost hurt the senses with the purity of tone. There was but one man, with long grey flowing hair and beard, standing alone in the cave's centre. He smiled at the visitor. "I knew you would return to find us, I knew the Hawk that circled above us carried your spirit within. Come, you will learn much about your journey, there are choices yet to make, you need to understand where and why others have failed, for you are not the first knight to set out on this quest, but I believe that your high ideals will guide you to be the one who will succeed."

For many hours Emrys talked, and the young knight listened to tales of myths and legends of long ago. The world around them changed, pale grew the light, as the colours dimmed to grey, the figures became mere shadows, floating on a misty sea. All warmth left their bodies until it seemed they would sink into despair, yet there was still hidden strength to be found. From deep inside him a flame flickered and grew, until he was bathed in a shimmering light that lit the way ahead, guiding him out of the watery cave to the shore above, fading in the glow of the moon.

He fell to the ground with a weariness he had never known before and sank into a dreamless sleep, from which only the light of the rising sun could restore his senses to consider all he had seen that night.

The sleeping Rhydian stirred with the warm sun that rose over the mountain peaks, bringing life back into his still body, as he began to waken the memories of last night filled his head. Stretching cramped limbs his hand touched something hard and cold. Rays of light shone with flashes of red fire that leapt out from its faded linen cloth. With care he unwrapped the cover, revealing the most beautiful sword ever made, its hilt covered in brilliant gems, garnets, rubies and emeralds. He ran his hand down the blade so smooth and cold to his touch, yet as he held it in his hand it felt light as he made sweeping strokes in the air.

"That sword was reputedly forged by the Elf smith Gofannon, for a king of great renown. It is called Caledfwlch" Looking at the speaker, he took a pace forward. "Sir Bedwyn, do you follow me? Your presence is strange. Tell me, whence comes this sword?" Looking on Rhydian with compassion and understanding he replied, "The Gwragedd Annwn brought me here to you, I do not doubt that they also laid the sword down beside you as you slept. It has not been seen for many years, hidden from man, whilst its renown spread far and wide." Rhydian's mind was troubled "It is a heavy burden for me to carry, by what reason have I been given this charge, for I am not worthy"

The old knight smiled wryly, "You have proven yourself worthier than others who held that sword, you can look at its beauty without the desire to own, this is why you have been chosen to return it and its scabbard to the rightful lord, in a place unknown to but a few, of whom I am one." Rhydian was thoughtful "I have seen such a place in my dreams, I believe that is where I must go" Quietly picking up the sword, he turned to bid Sir Bedwyn leave, yet found the place where he had stood now lay empty.

The suns shadows had grown long when Alain, keeping his watch by the camp, greeted Rhydian's return. "I had been told that you were nigh, your lady, my sister Gwen, sleeps now, I beg you leave her to rest. Since your departure she kept vigil not moving from this stream lest she lost you from her sight, twice I heard her call out, reaching down into the pool as if seeking to hold fast to I know not what. This dawn she smiled, said you were returning to us, then, Cyfaill beside her, she fell asleep." These words caused Rhydian to ponder, for twice, when under the spell woven in the watery cave, an extra strength had come to him, to fight the malaise which overcame him there.

The rays from the setting sun cast light over the sleeping figures, bathing them in a golden haze, creating such beauty that it filled his heart with unbearable pain. As he watched they stirred, drowsy with heavy slumber, in that uncertain world twixt sleep and waking, not sure of what their eyes tell them. With a cry of joy Gwen leapt up, as tears of pure happiness ran freely down her face they embraced. "I thought you were leaving me, I called to you, sending my love, but the water grew colder and I could feel you floating away to a distant place where I could not follow. Twice I lived your despair, I held your love closely as I fought to bring you once more to our world. As dawn broke this morn on the shore of a distant lake I saw you. Now you are returned, I am content. I implore you not to leave me again, but to take me with you, to share in any danger is far better than be left unknowing of your fate."

With a touch so tender he traced the salty channels on her cheeks. "You gave me the strength to resist the powers of the Annwn, though we travel across the length of our land, we will do it together, for all time. But enough I have much to tell you, Alain too" There in the grassy glade he told his story, as the dark of night fell and the firelight grew brighter, he took out Caledfwlch from its cover. The gleaming hilt shone, the stones reflecting the colours of the flames, its blade seemed to be a living being, quivering, yet icy cold to the touch. Gwen stared at it in awe, stretching her hand out towards it, then withdrawing it in fear. "This could ruin men's lives, it will demand from all who wear it their very soul. Made not with love, but with the desire to rule, the desire to own it will make even just and peaceful men become mad and cruel."

He then related the charge put on him to seek its scabbard and return them both to their rightful Lord. "I wondered long on why I was chosen, but if you are loath for me to continue, I will forsake my quest, and return to my father's land. Yet there must be a reason why it has been given to my charge." Alain then spoke, "The reason is that you see it, can admire its beauty, yet do not covet it. You have not taken another's life, following your own path without any desire for reward. Only such a person could safely bring the two parts together, then once united not use them to further their own cause."

Gwen smiled at her brother, for his wisdom far exceeded his years. Rhydian too looked at the young boy, "You give me pause for thought. I can, with your help, at least attempt to finish this quest, though where or how I will find the scabbard, I know not" Gwen laughed, "Be not concerned, for I fear it will find you, no matter where you may be" With a rueful laugh, Rhydian thought so too, for it seemed his adventures had befallen him, unasked. "Then let us sleep now, for we must continue northwards. The mountain paths are narrow, and steep, for a destrier this is a hard journey, Cadair is not built to traverse such mountains Bronn, who was born on the hills, has the agility needed to guide us over the ancient ways."

Chapter Twenty Two - Cymer Abbey

For a few days they rested in the glade, bathing Cadair's leg in the streams clear water, watching the pups as they grew stronger, until with eyes now open, they looked without fear at their new world, safe in Cyfaill's keep. In this peaceful place they drew closer together, with no need for other company. Laughter and tales shared, taking ever longer in the telling as the moon cast its silver light, bathing all in a shimmering glow. Soon the time came to leave, once more to resume their journey, leaving the low ground, taking the high pass northwards. Steady Bronn leading the way, pups snug on her back, watched over by Alain as he walked beside her, with Aldan's gift keeping them warm. Cadair followed finding the narrow pony paths hard to traverse. Rhydian watched his lady as she climbed with ease, she laughed at him, "You forget, I am well used to the hills, as children Alain and I ran like wild animals all day long, have no doubt, I can outpace you"

That night their bed was hard as they lay on granite rocks. Tired from their journey they slept together with the innocence of children, no dreams to disturb them, until woken by the morning sun to a sense of joy at just being alive, they continued onwards along the mountain ridgeway, until they started to descend, the path finally reaching the deep river valley where verdant meadows and deep lakes beckoned, beauty that enticed them to tarry. In such an idyllic place their pace slowed, stopping by the lake shores, in no hurry to reach the small town by the fording point of the river.

Rhydian drew Gwen close, saying softly "I want to savour these moments, good memories that I can lock inside my mind, to recover them when I am sad or afraid, a shield to protect my soul in times of darkness."

Gwen stood close by him, afraid to look into the water that ran beside her, least she saw visions of the dangers that surely lay ahead. They stopped for the night outside the town, at the edge of a wide flat meadow in the shelter of trees, out of sight of the houses.

As he slept, Rhydian dreamt. Once more he could see and hear strangers. Yet these people spoke a language he knew, the tongue of his birth. He felt many dangers abounded here, much anger and sadness too. These people were weary, in body and spirit. Soldiers stood guard, cruel whips cracked in their hands. All hope had gone; no fight was left within them. He tried to understand the words around him, but only one phrase reached him. "To enslave another human is to take away his humanity, yet I can raise my eyes to the hills and soar free as a bird in my imagination" These words were spoken by an old man, his eyes searching through the murky light, looking until he found the dream held Rhydian. Then satisfied, the old man lay down to sleep. When Rhydian awoke the air was full of mist and low cloud, water droplets hung on all. Quickly he stirred the others, and in haste they made ready to move. "I do not wish to stay here, we will stop instead at Cymer Abbey, I have a letter of introduction from Brother Thomas, I believe we will be safer there than if we stay in this doleful place."

The mist hung low as they forded the river, whilst the grey town still quietly slept. Making haste they took the wide river path towards Cymer Abbey. The sunrise crept over the valley, sending warmth to dispel the chilly air. It was but a short journey to Cymer where, lying under the watchful eye of a ruined hilltop castle, the Abbey began to stir, with sheep grazing amongst the cattle in the water meadows, black and white wandering peacefully in the morning sun lazily looking as Rhydian came into sight.

Their arrival was also noted by a brother, a strong swarthy man whose sombre face lit with delight when he saw the travellers. Hurrying to greet them in a loving embrace "I knew you would be here soon, Emrys sent word, come and break fast with me" Leading the way into the cobbled yard Ythel opened the stable doors, "You see, I have all prepared, the ci bach will be safe here, your hound can rest, she looks tired and has not much flesh on her." Rhydian laughed with pleasure, then he replied "Cyfaill will transfer her allegiance to you I fear, she has been sorely tried these last few weeks."

Later, when all the brothers left and were about their work, the repast finished, stories were told. Ythel's tale was simple, the abbey at Cymer had need of his skills and strength, so once his health was restored he left behind Ystrad Fflur and journeyed to this place, where, full in the Lord's glory he laboured to build the abbey church, caring for the animals and finding a peace, such as he had never known before, in this small loving community. Listening to the contentment in this Cornish wrestler's voice, Rhydian thought of the mysterious ways of the Lord. Desiring time and space for contemplation he left the others and followed the old track to the castle ruins sitting a' top of the hill.

Wandering amongst the scorched timbers, his mind heard the cries of anguish, shrill voices and fleeing footsteps as the flames surrounded them, with no choice but to stay and perish, or to fight and die in battle. Now beauty was all around, the grim play finished. Sitting on the cool grass, sleep and dreams visited him, so real he could touch the people who inhabited the land. A tall Roman, wearing purple on his hood, held a young maiden in his arms, gently stroking her hair and wiping tears away from her face.

"Weep not mine own Cariad, I have been granted permission, this day, by my noble father, to take you as my wife. He is not pleased, as the son of Macsen I should be following the campaign trail, seeking glory and taking a lady like Elen, my own mother, as my bride, not a slave girl from the mines, even though she has no compare in beauty or soul in this land." As the dreamer looked, he saw in the man's face his father's eyes, and in the girl's voice his melodic lilt, reaching across the years. As the dream faded it seemed that the love of long ago had taken away those fears still lingering around the castle mound.

Chapter Twenty Three –
A New Companion

Rhydian, returning to the Abbey grounds, watched with pleasure as Cyfaill's pups played, running on short wobbly legs, with excited sounds they explored, whilst keeping close by. Gwen was sitting on the grass laughing at their games, the biggest, boldest one, his coat as black as night, made darting attacks at her feet, until, suddenly tired, he returned to his mother's side to feed. Seeing Rhydian approach, Gwen gave a cry of delight, and making all speed reached his outstretched arms, a warm glow of contentment filling his being. As he held her close he remembered the two lovers of his dream, feeling certain that they were smiling down on him, sending their blessing across the years. Gently caressing her hair, Rhydian told his lady a story, of a slave girl's fears, and of the Roman noble who loved her. The evening star rose above the abbey as Ythel called them to enter within. "Our fare is plain, but there is plenty for all, tonight I have an old friend staying, he is eager to talk with you."

In the hall the fire cast long shadows with its glow lighting up the faces of those who sat in comradeship, they had no need for speech, simply sharing their meal and thoughts. Alone, in a quiet corner, a man sat, so still, he seemed not real, as if he was carved of stone, yet there was warmth, softness, all around him, that promised all whom he knew a safe haven to rest in. Rhydian found he was drawn towards this man by an invisible thread, binding them together for all time. The man looked up as they entered, beckoning "Ythel, my

Brother, come to me, I am desirous of speech with this young man. I have heard tales of his chivalry, of his skill with a Crwth that charms all, of a voice that assails the senses. I wish to meet this paragon of virtue to make my own judgement." His eyes shone with delight as his words caused discomfiture, with a flush of brilliant red suffusing his face, Rhydian laughed ruefully, and sat beside Ythel's friend.

After a short silence where he seemed to be coming to a decision, the stranger began to talk "My name is Gwyhyr, I have travelled far and wide over this fair land, now I intend to cease, just one more place to visit, one more demon to lay to rest, then I will roam no more. I go to Dinas Ffaraon, just a few days journey away, would you care to come with me?" The stranger bowed to Gwen, "If your lovely lady will grant me this pleasure" Gwen looked into the green of his eyes, then she replied "I have your measure, and so I give you my lord, guard him well, as your journeys are drawing to an end, so his have yet to run their full course" Gwyhyr smiled, "You have wisdom and beauty combined, to be cherished and protected, yet I see a courage that lies beneath, where no fear will hold you back from your chosen path, I pledge my life to those that you hold dear"

The two made preparations for their departure, Alain once more had care of Cadair, now Bronn too. Ythel took charge of Cyfaill and her pups, he was unsure if she would fret for her beloved master, so he sought Gwyhyr's advice, who reassured him, saying "Do not worry, I have spoken to the hound and she rests easy now. My friend, I have a fear, the times ahead seem to darken, yet I believe this young knight will bring a light to show us the way, maybe not a glorious flame but a steady glow that all can approach and feel its warmth without fear of burning. Not a name to live in men's dreams, but a base upon which the future of our children's children can be built"

As the morning sun rose over the hills the youth, Crwth slung over his shoulder, Rhydian felt a pang of guilt as he left his lady, yet he was eager to go and seek new horizons. "I give you my promise that wherever I go, you will be with me, tightly held inside my heart. I will return by the next rise of the new moon." Placing a soft kiss on her lips he waved goodbye, and strode out of the Abbey gate. Gwen watched until the two had vanished from her sight. Then, sitting under the shady tree, with a hound pup held closely, she let her tears flow.

The travellers soon left the Abbey far behind, a green track led them alongside the river's edge bounded on all sides by steep mountain slopes. Along one side ran a pale scar, creating a ledge wide enough for several men to walk abreast. As Rhydian looked along its length, he saw moving shadows, many people walking the dusty road. Listening intently he could hear voices drifting on the breeze across the valley. As if pulled by an invisible hand he left his companion's side and walked towards the sounds until reaching a mountain track, he stopped, eyes open wide, searching the bare hills. Doubt crept inside his mind, had those figures been a distant echo from a time long past, or a trick of the morning light? The way ahead was lit by the sun's glow as it climbed high in the sky, with a firm step he followed it, scarce noticing his companion once more walking beside him. They travelled in silence each one deep in their own thoughts.

Rhydian began to sing quietly, strumming the melody on his crwth, the notes floating on the wind until they were caught by the birds of the air, creating a concert of such vision that a blind man could see, music of such sweet intensity that even the deaf could hear. Gradually his song faded away, until it was only in the memory, where it would stay hidden 'til in some long time, yet to come it would rise again. Then to bring comfort, awake again the warmth that crept into ones soul, feeding the belief in immortality, giving courage and strength to journey on. Without a word being passed between the two men, one but a golden haired youth, the other who seemed as old as time itself, they continued down the road, each seeking their own truth.

That night they made camp by the side of the old road and as darkness fell each told a tale. Rhydian reliving the dream when he became a Hawk, how it felt to fly over hill and dale with sharpened senses and the freedom of the air. Then it was Gwyhyr's turn, struggling to find the words, as if he was unused to speaking, he told of knights from olden times, the kind of tales that passed away long winter nights gradually his voice seemed to change, taking a new, hypnotic, quality. Slowly as Rhydian's eyelids drooped, he slept. An Owl, swooping down on silent wings in the night sky, came to rest on the tree above them, calling to Gwyhyr with the understanding of an old friendship, man and bird, together as equals, without fear, using a common language, shared their minds.

Chapter Twenty Four – The Raven

The next day, as they walked the long track, a large black raven flew ahead of the two men the steady beat of its wings stirring the air as it rose high above the hillside. Its distinctive call seeking to greet the new day, it tumbled and dived as if full of joy, flying low over grass covered stone ruins, the like of others Rhydian had passed before. He could feel a bleakness here that frightens warmth away, yet seemed to beg him to tarry, promising wondrous secrets for him to discover. As he stopped, the raven turned and circled him, lower and lower he flew, reaching ever closer until his feathers touched Rhydian, urging him forward once more, until he was again matching Gwyhyr stride for stride towards a destination as yet unknown.

Far in the distance, flickering reflections of light from water held captive in a mountain lake created a rhythm, a dance that captured the rays from the sun bending them, curling them, then straight as a lance they spread across the land, with colour bursting forth, making each step he took lighter, the ground smoother. Drawing closer to the water he could see a house by the river's edge, with fishing nets around a small boat. A young woman, catching sight of them, called to her children taking them inside their home, barring the door. He could feel frightened eyes watching him, a baby cried suddenly, breaking the eerie silence, until just as quickly it stopped. The two men took rest by the lakeside, with Rhydian looking hopefully into the still water, praying that he be blessed with the sight of Gwen's sweet face, but he saw only his own reflection, which as he looked disappeared from sight.

A quiet voice spoke to him, yet he could see no one. The raven scratched in the fern clad hillside, its glossy black head tilted towards him, a beady eye glistened with all the ancient knowledge of its kind. The voice came again, and as he listened words formed inside his mind, "Look at me what see you there?" A long shadow grew beside him as the raven took wing and rose, high into the sky, it soared, faster and faster it flew. Rhydian, watching and turning, until his eyes could follow it no more, only seeing feathers, glowing in the sun's reflected rays.

One moment they shone with brilliant light, burnished until they were as red as sunset, then as quickly became pure white and for a moment, took another form, until across the sky, a dragon swooped, then gathering speed it vanished. A warm wind sprang up, and then, riding it, the raven returned, landing on the grass, a shiny jet black eye laughing with delight at the trick played on the watcher, who, unsure, looked back without understanding, but full of wonder.

The two men walked together in easy silence, with a friendship that belied the short days since they had first met. They took the old road high above the valley floor, following ways no longer trodden, all the time the raven kept them in his sight, circling, watching, calling with his harsh cry, that pierced inside Rhydian's mind, filling it with strange sounds, seeming to create words that he almost understood. He felt the birds intelligent gaze upon him, mocking him, daring him to a duel of wits, suddenly the bird soared upwards, until he became no more than a speck in the blue sky. For a brief moment Rhydian hardly moved, scarcely drawing breath, until, gathering himself together, he once more followed the track, taking his place beside Gwyhyr. "Tell me about the raven, why does he choose to come with us? At times, for no known reason, I have fear of him." Gwyhyr replied "I have known some of his kind who cannot be trusted; Menw is not such a one. He has been a true friend to me for many years, with much wisdom learnt from times long past, you can ever depend on him to come to your aid when needed."

They continued onwards, their paces evenly matched, they walked to a steady rhythm. Through wild moor land that could quickly change from quiet beauty to a savage beast as the rain and wind swept along the open tracks. A feeling of desolation descended upon Rhydian, chasing song from his heart, as if the cold reached inside his soul, slowing his steps until he came to a standstill. Far away he could see people gathering, shadows, the same as before. He could hear a low sound, the excited hum of anticipation spread towards him. Gradually he was pulled, inexorably, into that crowd, as if led by an unseen hand until he could move no more.

The crowds parted, revealing an amphitheatre, where games of war were played, with the winner taking the glory as many a brave man died. A young girl, heavy with child, tears running unchecked down her face, ran into the ring; she knelt beside a soldier, all her fears held in her being as she gently cradled him in her arms. He touched her face softly, "I have loved you above all things, hold that deep in your heart and place your trust in the Lord, I will find a way to guide you. My mother, the Lady Elen, will care for you and our child" His gaze seemed to rest on Rhydian, although no one there could see him, a smile of contentment lit his eyes as he gently let go of this life.

The shadows faded away until all had gone, with only a circle of grass where the strife had been and the wind the only sound. Rhydian shook his head, clearing the mists of time from within. He saw Gwyhyr waiting patiently for him to return to the present time, before resuming their journey once again.

Chapter Twenty Five –
A Perilous Journey

The track led onwards along the high ways, across wild heath land where only hardy ponies and sheep shared the solitude. The land before them dropped suddenly, streams gathered pace, cutting sharp paths into the land. Far in the distance the sea sparkled with reflected light from the sun, whose fiery brilliance turned the rivers below into molten lava flowing between wide yellow sandbanks, with high tree covered cliffs rising from estuary shores that towered upwards to the craggy mountain tops. Rhydian stood still in silent worship the beauty taking his breath away, Gwyhyr beside him, a bond of kinship held the two men, a sense of timeless knowledge.

As the sun sank gradually below the horizon, all colour faded away, the light becoming a memory until only shades of grey remained. "Tomorrow we will travel those rivers using the ebb and flow of the tides to take us on our journey, to traverse a dangerous passage, but it will save many hours of walking. Let us pray for a fair wind and a tranquil sea" The sun rose in the morn, a fair day promised as they made an early start. The path down by the stream was steep as it tumbled over rocks, eager to reach the river and then the sea. The deep ravine broadening until it reached the shore, where stood an ancient harbour.

Half hidden in a sandy cove, a coracle lay, its long oar resting, as if waiting for them. Gwyhyr smiled, "come my friend, be brave, although but a small craft, the men of Din-Gonwy have made it well, it will carry us with ease, take the aft seat, and keep watch for the changing currents" They were taken by the ebbing tide between the vast sand banks, along deeply cut channels twisting from side to side, passing small hillocks, sometime isles, with the open sea getting ever closer.

As they rounded the headland a wind sprang up, creating waves on the water. Using all his strength and guile, Gwyhyr steered a course round the headland, making for the river and quiet waters. Just when their safe haven seemed at hand a sudden gust lifted the slender boat into the whirling eddies of the sea.

The waves swept Rhydian into the cold water away from the Glaslyn estuary, far from the safety of nearby land. For all his youthful strength the tide had too great a pull, carrying him into the mighty ocean. As he prayed for courage he saw the black raven speeding towards him, wings held flat against his body the great bird dived under the waves, water sprayed Rhydian's face. Unable to see, he felt his body being lifted like a feather through the water. So fast did they travel he could not tell the manner of his rescuer, only feel the power and warmth of the body he rode.

They reached calmer, sheltered water here he saw the truth of tales told by sailors, for he was astride the back of a sleek dolphin. In awed voice, Rhydian spoke softly, "Menw, my friend, you are that most magical of beings, a shape changer, God did indeed send me help when I asked for it. I owe you my life, one day my debt will be repaid" Gently he slipped into the sea swimming for shore, watching as the coracle made headway through the sea, impatiently waiting to tell of his adventures, yet afraid his many questions would have no answer.

In the wide sheltered estuary, the flowing tide safely carried the coracle towards the pass where the river Glaslyn sped through its rocky gorge to the sea. The two travellers took the slim path winding beside the river as it gathered pace, fed by the streams falling down the mountainside. Spray covering them as they traversed narrow ledges of overhanging rocks, as they slipped on moss covered boulders, struggling to stay the course. Resting for a while with beauty all around them, Gwyhyr answered, with a smile, the faltering questions his young companion asked.

"I will tell you a tale from long ago to bring understanding of our friend Menw, who dwells in the shadows of time, one of the few who remain from an ancient race of people in the Western Isle, the domain of the children of Llyr, whose sorrow held sway for long years. The Eiddlig Gor took sanctuary in the caves, creating many fears with their dark looks and strong magical powers. Much mistrust abounded, Menw's people were hunted until only the strongest shape shifters survived, taking for safety to the water and air, keeping their true form hidden from all but a few.

But beware if you bring harm to their kind for they have long memories and long lives. Many years ago Menw had a young friend, although from different races they were boys together, both possessed of rare gifts, for which they were greatly feared. One day his companion was taken by the men of mighty Guorthigern, to the high mountains of Eryri, there to be an offering to appease the gods. The king believed the blood of a fatherless boy would bring strength and firm foundations to his fortress. Taking a raven's form Menw followed, keeping watch over his friend, through a great storm, over wild land. It was a hard flight for one so young, not yet grown fully into all his powers, during nightfall he rested close by, alone with his fears for what fate awaited them. Before the journey's end his agile mind had devised a plan, which he shared with his friend." Gwyhyr stopped to draw breath, "I will tell you no more of this tale until Dinas Ffaraon, where an ancient task awaits, in which we must not fail"

Chapter Twenty Six – Dinas Ffaraon

Reaching Bekelert they rested at a small Augustine Priory before setting out for Dinas Ffaraon, the end of their journey. A strong square tower sat on top of the rocky hill, from which flew the standard of Prince Llywelyn, a figure stood on the rampart walls, watching their approach. The raven flew over him, circling high before landing in the bracken that surrounded the fort, his presence giving Rhydian courage to face the Prince, then he and Gwyhyr crossed the bridge and entered the courtyard. Here they found only a small hunting party, a group of men enjoying the game abounding in this lonely place.

Rhydian was greeted with great pleasure and delight by Llywelyn, "My young minstrel, you are indeed a sight that warms my heart, I have much need of entertainment here, with none for company but these men, battle valiant but without knowledge of music, their only songs bawdy, tavern ditties, but tonight I will listen again to the beauty of your voice" Seeing his young guest searching the faces of his men, Llywelyn smiled, "My son Tegwared remains at Castell y Bere, soothing his hurt pride with another fair maiden, I trust your lady is well protected, she did not care to accompany you here, or is she, methinks, with child?" Laughing at the blushing youth, "Or have you not defiled her yet, is she still a virgin?"

Rhydian replied with quiet dignity "Until my quest is complete I will not marry my lady, then with the blessing of my parents and God we will become as one." The Prince replied "It is not my way, though I applaud your honour, but enough of this, bring your friend inside and tell me of your adventures since last we met, hide nothing in the telling" That night they fed well, the hunting company drinking until the early hours, until they sank into deep sleep, dreaming of home and the families they left behind, of the women waiting patiently for their return. As sleep to him came Rhydian heard Gwyhyr talking softly, an unknown voice replied, and somewhere in the distance a tormented soul cried.

In the morning Rhydian awoke, rising before all others, he walked to the lake, swimming in its cool clear waters he felt cleansed in body and mind. The rocky shoreline beckoned, enticing him to climb onto a carreg, rising from the cool waters. He could see a fine Eryr floated above him, riding the thermal air waves. Behind him tall trees grew thickly, concealing the entrance to a cave, just visible from where he stood, curious, he entered. A green light lit the inside, showing rough steps hewed into the side, wide enough for a youth to climb, leading upwards to the light source.

His slender frame belied the strength he possessed, and using this, he climbed the dark narrow steps, towards that light shining down from the top. Emerging from the shaft he found himself in a secluded glade, with no way out, bound on all sides by sheer, smooth, granite. As he walked away from the steps, towards the wall, a bell chimed from deep inside the hillside. Rhydian stretched out his hand to touch the surface, and as he did so a great rock slid back, revealing a stone bridge that spanned across a deep chasm, lit by soft candles, leading to cave containing a golden casket. Rhydian entered, prayers to God filled his mind, asking for the lord's guidance.

The casket opened as he approached, the brilliance of the gold contrasting with the plainness of its content;

there, lying on a cloth of silk, wrapped in a fragment of coarse linen, was an old, brown, leather scabbard. As Rhydian carefully held this, the casket wavered and then faded away. With the candle lights dimming he returned quickly over the bridge, tightly clasping the scabbard. The egress closed behind and he climbed down the steps to the cave, returning quickly to the fort, seeking Gwyhyr, eager to tell him the tale, sure that his wisdom would explain all.

Gwyhyr greeted Rhydian as he entered the main gate, "I have been watching for you, quickly, it is getting late and soon all will wake. You must hide your precious burden; its presence here makes me very anxious for your safety." Speedily they entered the chamber where Rhydian's belongings were spread out; his leather outer jerkin had the silken lining ripped at the seam. Slipping the scabbard inside, Gwyhyr carefully began stitching the garment, all the time talking. "Menw watched your adventure this morning, when he heard the bell and saw the door open, he knew that Myrdden's treasure casket would be found, the enchantment placed on the cave would only let a youth of pure spirit enter. Over time many men have sought in vain to find that entrance, they have bitterly fought and died in chasing the legend of riches that they believed lay under this hill. I need more time, events have moved too fast. Take heed of me, your story is best left untold"

The early morning sun was rising high, chasing the cold air away, as they approached the Prince and his retinue preparing for another days hunting. "Goodbye Menw, God speed and a safe return" Gwyhyr's words, softly spoken, almost a thought, floating on the wind, free as the bird they blessed, echoed in Rhydian's mind. He longed to ask questions, yet for now he must find patience. The Prince called to them, "you must hunt

with us Sir Rhydian, I will provide you with a mount."
Gwyhyr smiled at the eager face of his young friend,
"Go and enjoy the chase, but take note of this, I intend
to feast well tonight, be sure the twrch does not escape
you"

Seeking quiet, Gwyhyr climbed the walls, a plan
taking shape, a way for Rhydian to complete the task he
had been set. How difficult that would be, what
temptation to be met, was still unknown. Over long
centuries many others tried, valiant men, but without a
true purity of spirit, had failed.

Chapter Twenty Seven – Farewell

That evening in the great hall there was much merriment the twrch was slowly turning on the spit, voices, strident in their efforts to be heard, vied with each other, telling tales of the chase, each story growing, with much vying among the knights, of their bravery and the tracking skill that lead them to the prey, until, glorying in the final kill they returned home, bone weary and ready for the feast.

Rhydian joined in the fun, yet as he looked at the beast he felt sadness, but took comfort that it was his keen sword thrust that had ended the struggle, a swift and clean end to a worthy opponent.

"Come minstrel boy, bring memories of the ladies we left behind, you must sing for your ale tonight" The Princes' words were echoed around the room, until amid cheers, Rhydian was lifted onto a wooden table. Laughing he began to sing, bawdy songs, ballads, childhood rhymes that all joined in, until he could sing no more. The Prince applauded, then called to Gwyhyr, "I know of you, that many a tale you have told to while away the long winter's nights, tell us the legend of this place. I know it well, as a child I oft have listened and many is the hour that I spent searching for dragons."

"I will gladly re-tell the old tale, there are many versions, mine is one not well known, yet methinks it may be nearer to the truth than others" His figure seeming to grow taller as he began to speak. He retold the familiar, ancient tale of how a mighty ruler, a fierce fighter in battle, could fail to build a castle that stood upright. His listeners knowing full well the story cheered the Red Dragon as it vanquished the white

Saxon intruder, yet fell silent at the final twist, for Gwyhyr told a different ending.

"Out of the mist emerged the victor, his red scales reflecting the fiery tongues of flame he blew at those gathered close by. The boy, Ambrosius, turned to Guorthigern addressing him and his men.

'You must leave this place, no building will stand here for many years, take the road westwards to the Llŷn, there you will find a hill, looking outwards to the sea on all sides. Here will be your new fortress where your people can live in safety, but sacred fires shall descend until you are consumed and your sons will rule a divided realm. My knowledge of the dragons is from the past, this is of the future. Your line will pay homage to a king, whose name will live 'til doomsday.'

That night Guorthigern sought out Ambrosius, intending to slay him, in fear of his prophecies. As he was entering the bedchamber he heard laughter, the joyous sound of children playing. He watched as one turned round and round, too quickly for Guorthigern's eyes to follow. The boy changed colour, red, white, green and yellow until it seemed there was not just one child, but four. Suddenly he stopped, and looked towards the door. Ambrosius called out,

'Enter, Come and meet the red Dragon of Cymru, but be careful, he has not yet fed, with his help we shall be able to foretell your future'

As he watched, the small, unknown boy grew in stature, changing shape, growing wings and a long, sinuous, tail his red scales glowing with fire. With a frightening wail the brave warrior king turned and fled from the room. As the dawn rose on the following day, an air of gloom lay around as Guorthigern ordered all his men to leave.

'I will go to the Llŷn, there to build my Caer, I believe this Dinas now belongs to Ambrosius, it is forever his stronghold'

This is the true ending to my story" Finishing speaking Gwyhyr sat down, his tale now told.

That night, when the Prince and all his men lay sleeping, Rhydian thought deeply on Gwyhyr's tale, wondering at this new version of an ancient legend. He believed that last night the Prince had not been the intended audience, but that the story had carried a message for him to hear and understand. A truth from an age long past, awaiting the time when all could finally be completed, and set free from their earth bound prison those restless spirits, for now he was sure who his travelling companions were.

He did not see yet why he was chosen, nor how he could complete this venture. He almost felt angry, that it was not meet to place such a burden upon him, and yet a feeling of great pride surged through his body, he rejoiced in his fate for was he not a knight and had he not wanted to prove his worthiness? He thought of Gwen, of his deep love for her, and as sleep took him he held her smile fast in his heart. Waking renewed, the events of the past day fresh in his mind, he sought Gwyhyr. He found him on the Dinas walls, searching the sky southbound. "My good friend what do you seek in the heavens?" "I look to Menw's return, for you must leave these bastions quickly, but I am loth for you to go until all is in place for the next part of your journey."

Rhydian turned to face Gwyhyr – "Are you leaving me? I need your guidance now more than ever" The reply he received brought no ease to his mind "I say to you, your conscience will guide you better than I, for I have lived on this earth too long and am weary. A keen and virtuous youth will find the right solution to a centuries old problem, created by mans desire, with spirits held in thralldom until released by a pure soul that is as yet untouched by greed and selfishness. Fear not, all have not fled from your side, I see Menw approaches, let us greet him" A raven swooped down, landing at their feet, his beady eye held Gwyhyr's, exchanging a silent message.

"We must find the Prince, and ask for safe passage out of his lands, now your quest moves to its close. We will accompany you until those that you chose are again at your side, for Menw has safely guided your lady over the mountains, which held no dread for her, she would make a truly worthy knight!" At this news Rhydian could not contain his delight he looked for Menw, but he was high in the sky speeding back to his charges, to bring them safely to the Bekelert Priory, there to wait for Rhydian before they began their final trek, united again.

Part Five

To
The Llÿn

Chapter Twenty Eight – The Reunion

The two companions made ready for their departure before seeking out the prince, Rhydian felt no wiser about their next step, nor understand the urgency for the hurried leave. "My friend, you fear for me yet do not tell me why, I am not a coward, unable to face dangers, I must know what manner of battle awaits me so that I may prepare" Gwyhyr thought for a moment, then he spoke, "You have the right to know what you have in your keeping and why it is sought, give me you dagger, I will show you the powerful treasure you carry and then you will be mindful of its danger" Taking the blade he cut deeply into Rhydian's arm, who, startled at this seemingly wanton attack drew back, unsure, his trust faltering.

"Look at the wound Rhydian, you must take note, then hold your silence, many would kill you if it was known Caledfwlch's scabbard had been found. You need to take the two parts to a place of safety, holy ground, where hearts are pure and desire for worldly power absent." From the cut, he saw no blood, whilst a pleasant warmth ran up his arm. As he looked in awe the skin healed, leaving no scar, no sign to show where the knife had been. "As long as you wear this coat with its hidden burden, you will not fear any blade, without it, you are once more alone"

For one moment Rhydian felt the desire to own the sword and scabbard for himself, for surely he could conquer all others, become the mighty knight of his dreams, he would seek and find the grail. But the knowledge came that to him, a mere mortal, such power was too great, the temptation too high, its possession would destroy the soul, so with a sigh he took off the jacket, turning away from such glory. "We shall now depart from here, you weave stories of enchantment where reality and fable entwine."

Carrying all their belongings they left to seek Llywelyn, as they passed, a figure emerged from the shadows, following them into the Dinas keep. His pale, sallow, features twisting with an unholy smile, he seated himself amidst the prince's men as they gathered together before the days hunting. Gwyhyr strode towards the high table; his long cloak bellowed out behind him, as they approached men gave way, granting them access.

"My Lord, we crave your permission to continue on our journey west. We fain to leave your company and so request your blessing as we leave, no longer to remain, to grant us safe passage across your domain." After a long thoughtful silence the Prince replied, "You have my leave, to all men I say woe betide any who harms you or yours whilst on the land I rule. I do not hold sway in the Llŷn; my hand cannot protect you there. Before you leave I have need of talk with you, in truth I believe you are more than at first appears."

Suddenly he arose, "It is my wish that I shall accompany you to Bekelert, I have not been there for a long while, it is time I laid to rest my sorrow, the wrong of years ago cannot be changed, but in such a place one should rejoice, not avoid. With your good grace we will go now, the hunting can await another day" As Rhydian and Gwyhyr tried to hide their concern and dismay they went out into the sunlight, where the Prince was issuing orders, in preparation for his absence," I will return tomorrow, for the journey is but short enjoy a day of leisure, there will be time yet for sport."

The three men walked in silence alongside the Glaslyn river, rejoicing in the solitude and peace of the hills, with heather clad slopes and tall trees bending down to the waters edge, white foam broke over the grey stones, creating a ledge for the travellers to walk along. Stopping to take a drink the Prince spoke to Gwyhyr "I have great cause to think since I met with you, your tale of olden days, of legends from our past, carried the ring of truth, as of old friends that you knew, yet how could that be, for many centuries have past since the all mighty Guorthigern and his armies lived in these lands. Our young knight, whose journey began at my command, now carries an aura of destiny, the carefree boy has become a man in so short a time."

"He has but one more mountain in his journey to climb, if he succeeds where others have failed, and lays to rest sorely tried souls, then his quest will be most blessed, and an inspiration to all that come after. I have belief in his integrity, but fear that greed may make a thief of others." Gwyhyr looked full hard into the eyes of Llywelyn, who filled with anger, began to rise and turned towards the older man. "Do not measure me against other men, whatever your fears, I assure you nothing is great enough to tempt me to become as a common varlet, I will not take of their own from any man, not even if the fabled Myrddin's treasure had been found"

Suddenly he ceased, a look of pure delight crossed his face, "The cave under the hillside, waiting for a fair-headed youth, many's the time I've tried to find its hidden entrance, listened for its bell to toll yet never found the door. I beg you, tell me the whole story" He listened intently as Rhydian related the story, telling how he found the cave where was held the gaudy casket and its simply wrapped contents, how, leaving the gold untouched, he had taken the scabbard to Gwyhyr, who foretold the dangers it would bring. So intent were the three they did not hear a sharp intake of breath from the tree lined banks behind them, nor see the figure of a man hidden in the shadows. "And now my friends, what plan do you have for your precious burden? You are entrusted with a sacred bequest, if this is known you will be hunted to your death." Rhydian replied with simplicity "I put my faith in God that he will guide me to safety and show me the final resting place to hide the sword and its scabbard. But enough, I see the raven flies overhead, 'tis time to move onwards to where Gwen awaits us."

They continued down the river bank, each man deep in thought, taking the steep path out of the ravine, unaware of the man who followed. Swiftly they passed through Bekelert, reaching the Priory as the bell called the few to prayer, as their shadow, drawing closer, kept tight to the walls, they reached the entrance, here Rhydian beheld a sight that caused him to laugh out loud.

A boy chased three hound pups round a destrier, belongings were strewed around a pack pony, with panniers resting under her belly, there contents fallen on the grass under the shade of a tree. Before the wind could blow them further, a young maid tried hastily to retrieve them, whilst the playful pups carried them to far parts of the Abbey grounds. "See my Lord what manner of army this knight leads, a fabled sword could not have a more unlikely guard" At the sound of his voice Gwen turned and ran with the hound Cyfaill towards him. Cadair whinnied, and pulled young Alain over, as, he too, headed towards Rhydian, who was knocked to the ground in the assorted mêlée.

Llywelyn bent down to pick up a pup from the fray, "You have the finest followers any could wish for, I envy you them. I would that others looked to your choice of companions. The cenau are strong and bold, this one reminds me of my Gelert, whose tale I told you before." His hand caressed the soft head, sorrow bringing a tear to his eye. Rhydian smiled "My lord, he is yours, allow me to present him to you, his sire is of great Phinn's lineage, his dam here saved my life with her brains, so he is worthy to be a Prince's friend." With order restored once more they entered the Priory cloister.

Chapter Twenty Eight – Making Ready

The quiet of the hall was broken by the excited voices of reunited lovers, exchanging tales and gentle kisses, with the greeting of old friends and making new, until finally ceasing, when peace descended once more to the Priory. Rhydian watched Cadair and Bronn grazing on the banks of the Glaslyn, caressing Cyfaill's head as he gave thanks for the safe arrival of his beloved friends, wondering if he had the right to ask them to continue, for leading them to the journeys end would bring many dangers. Deep in thought, he remained unaware of the stranger's footfall behind him, unheeding of his hound's warning. He returned to his friends with the evening sun setting below the mountain, bathing the Priory in a crimson glow, as if the very stones were afire, a true beacon to all who travelled the lonely roads.

The low murmur of voices sounded in his ears, coming from the arbor where the scent of herbs lay gentle on the warm air. Sitting on the grass at Gwen's feet, with his fair head gently resting on her knee, Rhydian began to talk to his Prince, of his adventures, how Cyfaill and Cadair rescued him, the meeting with Alain and Gwen, his flight as a hawk. He told him of his joust, of the shame he felt when he failed in the last moment of victory, unable to land the final blow. Of truth intermixed with fable.

As he drew to a close, his eyelids drooping in sleep, he said to Llywelyn "I place my trust in you, to keep these words close, and if I fail in my final task, I plead that you take care of my Lady." At these words Gwen spoke "There will be no need I would not leave your

125

side, for together we journey. I know not where you are going, but you go with me"

Llywelyn looked at Gwen, a smile crossing his face, "I give you my word, I am honoured that I have a place in your story, it is a sacred charge. I will not fail you, none shall hear from me of your precious treasure, nor do I covet it. I have received a greater reward, that of your friendship. But take heed, you must guard well the burden you carry, until the Annwn once more have it in their keeping." Turning towards the door the prince entered the Priory, his new pup held tight in his arm. "Before we retire, one thing worries me; I hope no harm has come to the smallest pup, for only three arrived here." Alain answered him "Do not fret, she is well, but still small. She is in the care of Ythel, he loves her dearly and she is safe with him."

They all returned to their rooms unaware that a slim figure emerged from hiding and stood in the shadow staring at the windows of the Priory. A look of anger crossed the man's face; his thoughts were black *"I now will follow your every step until I can at last take my revenge for deeds of long ago. My forefather suffered and swore one day to return to reclaim that which was rightfully his. I will redeem that oath, so that all shall see the truth!"*

Once inside the Priory, Llywelyn held fast to Rhydian, keeping him back, "Take heed of this, there is a knight; his name is Medraut, that travels with my company. I care not for him, for methinks he is not trustworthy, although he comes from an ancient line. This morning he asked me many questions, where you were born, who you father is, why you travelled as a commoner with such strange company, I gave him no answer. You must hide well your treasures, for I am minded this man has some knowledge, you are forewarned"

In the quiet of his room Rhydian took his coat, ripping it open to remove the leather scabbard, placing this deep in the bottom of Bronn's pannier, curling it under a hessian cover. Over this he laid Aldan's blanket, making a soft bed for the pups to lie on. He pondered about the sword Caledfwlch, it must be concealed, but how?

Taking his Crwth, he bound the sword tight against its back, the blade lying flat along the upright bar, then lashed it firmly to the plain saddle roll that would lie across Bronn's broad back. Taking his own sword he wrapped this in plain cloth, its shape telling all what lay within, this he placed openly on his own bundle, which Cadair carried. The sunlight of dawn lit up the hall before, satisfied, he finished, and he laid down to sleep, his mind filled with concern for that in his keep.

Next day they bade farewell to Prince Llywelyn, who looked longingly at the small group. "I would go with you, but I must return, for within my knights are many who wish to take my place. If I am gone for long, you would see another face ruling my land. May God's blessings go with you" They watched him leave, the small body of his new hound tucked inside his jacket. A feeling of great sadness filled Rhydian; it was as if a heavy weight was pulling down his heart.

Gwyhyr remained at the Priory with Menw, and now, as he needed guidance more than ever, he was left wanting, and alone, where were his mentors now? Then he felt a soft hand slip into his, and laughed, for how could he be lonely, with Gwen and Alain by his side? Together with his horse and hounds they would ride through any storm that approached, showing no fear or doubt and grow in love and stature without peer.

Chapter Twenty Nine –
Towards The Llŷn

Rhydian scanned the blue sky hoping for sight of a black bird high in the sky circling right above them, striving to hear the harsh craa of its call, but in the air all was still for as far as he could see. They followed the Glaslyn as it flowed to the open sea close by, the Llŷn, that narrow strip of land pointing westward to their journey's end. The path was hard and narrow, rocks, slippery with wet moss underfoot, letting only the surefooted across. They left the riverside, climbing higher to seek an easier way, where Cadair's great physique and Bronn's heavy load could move with speed in safety, continuing onward, with no need for rest.

The valley's beauty spread out before them, the bright, crashing water creating a roar as it fell down waterfalls, which could be heard from their lofty pathway. Above a lonely bird, like a sentinel, pointing to where the distant sea beckoned tempting the river onwards, to bravely enter the big ocean tides, never more to tumble over the mountains of its youth. Reaching a coastal track they descended to the moryd, where a bridge crossed onto flat, fertile land over a sandy ridge.

Here lay small boats waiting for the next tide, fishermen watched the strangers as they arrived, warily at first, then seeing no threat, in friendship. Children laughed at the pups as they began to slip down Bronn's back to run free, their legs, cramped from the long confine of the pannier collapsed, leaving them at the mercy of small hands eager to catch and hold them tight.

Through the laughter came a louder voice, asking to know from whence the party came, and to where they travelled hence. A tall figure walked towards them, by his bearing a true man of the sea, his skin bronzed with living under the sun, eyes gazing from a weather-beaten face, Rhydian knew that here was a leader of men. "We travel to the Llŷn, firstly to Borth-y-Gest where my lady's father set sail to lands unknown, to the fair country that Prince Madoc found. Her brother sailed too and has ne'er been seen again, she has desired to see once again the place from which they left."

The man stared long at Rhydian, "That is but the heft of the tale, I choose to ask no more, for I can judge a man's worth, now eat with us, do not begrudge me the pleasure of your company, I become lonely for new tales." That day they were treated as royalty, a feast prepared from the sea, cooked on an open fire washed down by homebrewed ale, none could desire better company. At Gwen's behest, Rhydian began to sing until the night drew in and reluctantly children, hiding from sight, were gathered up and an evening of magic ended.

From afar a man watched, his mind becoming sick with envy at the easy camaraderie with which Rhydian made friends, his heart filled with bitterness and poison with the desire to take from him that which he valued and held dear. He would bide his time, until unguarded, he would take the treasures and regain his rightful place as a Prince in the land his forefathers once ruled, erase the wrongs of years ago. Keeping these thoughts close he settled down to the dark sleep where shadow blows the daylight away, and so creates frightening dreams.

The dawn broke to a grey and dismal day, no beams of sun broke through the mist curling in from the sea, hiding the water's edge from view, where the boggy land could entrap an unwary traveller holding tight until the tide turned, and so be lost forever from sight. "Keep close to the hillside, do not stray off the shore and you will be safe. Follow the land, it may take more miles, but guideless, the Treath must not be crossed" With this warning the fisherman bid farewell, tossed his nets into the boat and set sail.

Taking good heed of his words the small party left, Cyfaill took the lead her keen nose testing the air and her innate instinct choosing the right path. Following them, as if linked by an invisible cord, came the lone knight. Running quickly and easily, the many years of hard training had given him speed and endurance, and so he kept them well in sight. By noon they had reached Pen Morfa, where they stopped to rest, yet an uneasy fear held Rhydian, he could not be still. "I must see what lies beyond, this place holds old knowledge crying out to be heard, with words in a language I can feel but not understand"

He rode Cadair fast away, to a hilltop, where trees grew thickly, past green meadows, until he entered a grove of oak where mistletoe hung from branches like a cloak behind which no birds sang. Dismounting he stood straight, his eyes closed, and mind open. A flood of voices rang in his ears, chanting incantations, entering his senses, no longer words, but emotions, pure feelings that overcame him. Suddenly all ceased and a soft silver light took the shape of an old wizened man who held out his hand to Rhydian, as they touched he felt a cold fire spread through his body, he watched as the light curled around him, until the two were as one.

Slipping into a deep sleep the sound of song had begun to enter his spirit, unknown words from an ancient past, bringing peace and tranquility, yet full of power, a fast flowing stream washing over him, cleansing his mind. While he slept time seemed halted, he saw unconfined across the years from beyond the grave to the distant future, feeling the common thread that bound all sentient beings.

Slowly he woke, with Cadair standing guard, his sweat drenched sides heaving; his eyes full of fear, yet no thought of leaving his beloved master entered his being. Rhydian reached out to touch his friend, with new understanding, no more doubt of his chosen course. He had been given the courage to continue onward, to reject the temptation of great power that few could resist. As he approached Pen Morfa the sun broke through, as if the heavens rejoiced in new found hope.

They soon reached Borth-y-Gest, the road was easy and untroubled, here the small harbour was busy with boats of all sizes. Some being large enough to sail to far distant lands, whilst others were small, frail craft, built for skimming over the marshlands, their flat keel drawing little water, propelled by poles that skillfully saw them glide among the reeds, hunting the wildfowl, laying traps for unwary game to bring home.

Gwen looked around her, brow furrowed as she recalled that day from her past, when she had fled from her mother's side, clasping her brother tight, pleading with him to stay, not to leave that night. She could feel still her father's arms, iron strong, as he pulled her away, then carrying her the boat's length, placing her harshly in Aldan's embrace. In her despair she wept, tears running down her face she watched her beloved Bron leave her life forever.

Now she stood in the same place, a younger brother at her side. "You were but a babe, I was not unkind, I loved you full well, but I would have left all behind to go with them. Our mother would not leave you, nor this land, and I was only a girl-child. I often rued this day, but no more, for I have found an abiding love in my Rhydian, and in you, Alain, I could not have a better, truer, brother. I thank you for bringing me here, I have chased away the demons, they now flee my life forever" Then turning away from the harbour she sat on a low wall gazing far along the foreshore.

Rhydian knelt at her feet, "I cannot promise that your life will one of ease, of wealth I have nothing, I am poor in all but love, but this I swear, as long as there is breath in my body I will hold your heart in mine, until my death" Gwen gently touched his face, "I want no earthly riches for I have the wealth of friends, so no more speeches, whilst the sun is still high, we will take the road west and move on, for we have yet to complete our quest"

Leaving the harbour behind they climbed the headland where they could see to the distant horizon. Like a hand, the Llŷn pointed their way, disappearing into the misty clouds that hung over the high hills. They saw the newly built walls of Llywelyn's castle perched on top of a small hill, almost an island, across the bay, the twin towers, tall and strong, stood their guard. The party, keeping a goodly distance from the castle, followed the path of the saintly Cadfan to the Isle of Ynis Enlli, where many had found solace and healing after crossing the treacherous sound from Aberdaron. They met with other travellers along the way, stopping at St Cawrdraf's church, here a throng of pedlars greeted them, selling sweetmeats and fairings.

Rhydian, aware of the dangers that such a crowd brings, carried on without stopping until they came to a quiet place by a river. In the balmy evening, with the warm fire light casting a glow around the makeshift camp, they rested. "I dreamt I was a hawk that flew high above this blessed land. Down below I saw the sea on either side of a crest of hills that ran down to its tip. I saw a fort, holding fast to the stone covered moors, I felt drawn to that place as if someone was calling to me - now I wish to retrace my flight and find the fort once more. We must leave the Pilgrims Way and take the inland path, for I believe that on that lonely hill there are answers to be found."

As they slept on in peace, their watcher made no sound to show his presence, biding his time until he was ready to act. That morn they left the flat coastal plain for hilly moors, which offered no cover for their shadow to hide. He was content to stay back, keep to the lower hillside for he knew they had to descend the ridge on route to the Island, watching, as they searched for the fort.

Chapter Thirty - Carn Fadryn

The bleak moorland that covered Carn Fadryn contrasted with the green fertile land below; from its wind blasted summit Rhydian saw the world beneath lie like a picture, splashes of green and yellow, encircled by the sea, pure blue flecked with white. Behind him Eryri's tall mountains reached to the sky. Southwards, rivers met the ocean's waves as they flowed into the wide bay. Beyond the distant horizon lay the land of the Tuatha-de-Danann, an ancient people whose spirits live on in the otherworld. Ruined walls lay all around, where a mighty fort had once stood; they call out to those who will listen, telling of the hopes and fears of times past, now and the future, memories of forebears that lie deep within the soul.

Gwen moved beside him with the cool air causing a shiver to ripple along her slim body, his thoughts returned to shelter before the night drew in. Together they found a place, where, as the light began to fade they made camp, the fire created shadows, giving life to the stones around them. As the moon rose a plaintive song drifted on the breeze, waking Rhydian from fitful slumber.

Following the music he saw a man standing on the ridge, staring out to sea, where a great wave thundered over an unknown land, a watery fate descending on Maes Gwyddno. As he watched the sea appeared to move with the song, when, from the briny foam, burst forth horses, pure white and glistening under the moonlight, so swift they outran the sea, the thunder of their hooves awakening the sleeping villages, calling them to flight. As he listened the song was changing, becoming faster, louder and more urgent, a cry of despair torn from the man's soul. As if in answer to this prayer a black bolt descended from the sky, wings held tightly to its side, and the familiar sight of a raven dived into the sea, disappearing in the maelstrom.

A horse, black as jet, galloped out of the water, eyes like the yellow sunset staring from his giant head. Flying fast over the ground, he came to a lonely dyke, where a great earth mound bravely held back the incoming waters. Like a cauldron, a deep well boiled and churned, here a young maiden stood by the wall, tears of shame flowing down her face as she tried to mend the breaking bank. From this place the horse took her, running to the far distant high land where, exhausted, he sank to the earth. From the upland she looked on in sorrow, as all but a few were drowned, overcome by the crashing sea. From his hill a spell bound singer cried bitter sweet tears, his song now a low lament for the lost.

The dawn slowly broke, returning the present to the hilltop where Rhydian stood. At this time the Annwn is close to those who open their eyes and hearts, too soon the portal closes, but for a moment, standing in a gateway, two figures looked across time, their love speeding its way, enfolding him in peace. As the vision faded he wondered at its meaning, of questions that needed to be answered.

As the morning sun rose over the windblown hilltop Rhydian wandered slowly among the rocky outcrop, his thoughts still with the visions of the night before. In the distance, where the land ran into the sea, he saw a green island that beckoned him, surrounded by white flecked waves dancing over the water. A shaft of light lay across the flat fields below, as if pointing the way, a sign, or mayhap a portent from a watching Faye.

135

Turning to go, his foot caught a fallen stone bringing him to his knees. He brushed the dust away revealing ancient carvings, half broken fragments of forgotten words.

Hic jacet, here lies, *pace*, peace, as he read understanding came to him, *Matercula*, little mother, the names *Sevira* and *Modrom*, he could see another word, still clear – *liberta*. A caressing warmth spread up his arm, entwining itself in his heart, a pure thread of love reaching across the years. "Be easy my Roman soldier, the Lady Elen took care of your child, you can rest in peace now." Then with a light spirit he returned to his lady, ready for the next part of the quest, renewed in vigour and purpose, eager to continue on the journey.

They descended the steep hillside to level ground, where, waiting patiently; their lone watcher was biding his time, ready to strike. Rhydian charged Alain to make camp in the lush meadows yonder, where the grazing and water was plentiful, and then he took Cyfaill hunting. They set a quick pace until soon out of sight, after an hour of good hunting they rested, the sunlight warming them they began to doze. Suddenly the hound gave tongue, waking Rhydian, with one great bound she was flying back to camp, all other thought chased out of her mind. As he followed he heard the raised, fearful call of Cyfaill, urging him forward. Nearing the place of their parting he saw Alain, so still, he feared for his life, Bronn stood guard, then a pup began to whine. Rhydian searched, but of Cadair and Gwen there was no sign. Rhydian tended to Alain, washing the blood from his face desperate to know what had happened at this place, praying for life to return to the motionless body.

Slowly Alain began to move, his unfocussed gaze staring blindly upwards. The fog began to lift from his mind and words tumbled out "He has Gwen and Bronn is hurt, the sword's thrust slashed her deeply. I tried, but he was too strong I failed you" Tears welling unchecked, he took a long sobbing breath. Rhydian looked hard at Bronn, but there was no sign of a wound, just the faintest of marks, a pale white line across her chest. "She still wears her panniers, fear not the scabbard protects all living creatures, and now tell me what has befallen Gwen"

Alain stumbled over his words as he began his tale "You had no sooner gone from sight than a man appeared, so silent and swift, I did not fight, there was no time before he held Gwen, I was afeared he would harm her. The pup bit him, then Cadair reared and in the melee Gwen broke free, falling to the ground she hit her head and lay still, I tried to move, but found I could not, it was as if my legs were held tight, bound together by fear. By the time my courage had returned it was too late, he stood over her, his sword unsheathed. Then without thought I ran at him, but he only laughed at me and thrust me away, then he slashed Bronn, I saw blood flowing and flew at him, I remember no more."

Rhydian looked at Alain, and laid his hand on his shoulder "Be not ashamed for many men, well trained and older than you, know what it is to be powerless, unable to move when the heat of battle descends." Standing deep in thought, the beat of his heart pounding hard in his body, he pondered his next move. "We must follow them, the tracks lead towards the sea, but I do not understand, I am the only one who Cadair will obey, then why has this man freely taken him?" Alain saw the look of pain, of betrayal, on Rhydian's face. "He has gone with Gwen, a loyal guard to protect her, see also, a small dog's paw prints following them; Cyfaill's son is a true warrior methinks. She'll have no

137

trouble tracking them, we can travel fast" Rhydian began to smile, with his spirits lifting at last.

Chapter Thirty One - The Rescue

Rhydian removed Aldan's blanket from Bronn's pack, placing it around the shivering Alain's slender back. "Your mother's love will give protection, her courage will sustain you in whatever lies ahead, her knowledge of healing is an ancient craft from an ancient people" From its hiding place he took Caledfwlch, "The fable of this sword grew in my mind throughout childhood I dreamt of wearing it into battle, now when I should, I feel a strange reluctance, for I fear it has a malignant power that may overcome me. But I must not cower behind my fancies" With sword and scabbard united once more, they followed Cyfaill as she eagerly sped after the trail, heading west towards the setting sun, with Bronn carrying her burden steadily towards the barren slopes of Mynydd Rhiw.

The sky burned like a fiery furnace, a crimson land surrounded by a golden sea out of which rose a dark brooding hill. Rhydian halted Bronn, and softly called Cyfaill to his side, he pointed to where figures could be seen, sheltering in the lee of the hill "You must bide here, I will travel quietly alone" Alain began to protest "I wish to go alongside you, for she is my sister" Understanding, Rhydian smiled "I may not succeed in the task, you must keep a vigil if I fail, take up the challenge. Who knows what peril lies in store. Cyfaill will stay here also, her keen senses will tell you if help is needed, for I make no pretences to fighting skills, I may yet call you to my assistance"

Alain watched as they vanished into the distance sadly he settled down to wait, unsure of his desires, should Rhydian succeed alone? Or should his squire's help be asked for? Stroking the soft coat of his puppy as she slept beside him he began his long vigil, barely breathing, making no noise, listening for the call to glory that would give him a high place in a true knight's story.

The evening sky glowed as if Beltane's fire lingered as the last rays of the setting sun threw bright red layers over the menacing hills, slowly fading into half-light, until the cool silver moon washed it anew. Into this shadow land Rhydian slipped, his mind taking control, stilling the beating heart, to find a route to take, unseen, towards the menacing slopes of Mynydd Rhiw. There in the lingering light he saw Gwen, she sat so still and quiet that he feared for her safety, he was beset with self doubt, was he truly a brave knight fit to rescue his lady? Did he have the right to wear the sword of destiny?

He watched as across the scene a tall dark figure moved, in his hand was Rhydian's own sword, now loose of its cover. In great anger he raised his voice and approached Gwen. At this Rhydian, all caution forgotten, started forward, he began to quicken his pace, calling her name, sending a warning to her captor. The man turned round, facing the oncoming youth with a smile of anticipation on his lean face. He spoke softly, "I was certain you would follow, I will take that which is rightly mine, you fooled me once, but not again, I see Caledfwlch by your side, no doubt that shabby scabbard is what I seek also. Come here my pretty boy and I will show you how a real man can fight"

Rhydian stood very still, keeping Gwen in his sight, answering softly "You are not the first to call me boy come closer and find the truth, for it will give me joy to prove you wrong, you have done harm to those I hold dear, for this you must pay." They drew close, each wary to strike first, Medraut's sword flickered like a silver tongue, as his practised eye measured the distance between them, his lithe body swaying as he circled around the younger knight, standing so still, biding his time, content to wait, the great Caledfwlch, heavy in his hand, seemed to pulsate with power, urging him to fight. Then, with a sudden move he lunged forward, fighting as if a demon lived inside his body, until time itself stood still. He forgot where he was or who he was, until, with his enemy lying helpless at his feet, he raised his arms above his head, a red mist glazed his eyes and he stood poised for the final thrust.

As the arm descended, Medraut felt the last of life slipping away, eyes closed, he waited. He did not see the gentle hand that stayed the blow, nor hear the soft voice of calm cooling the battle fired mind with its balm. Slowly feeling the madness of rage depart, Rhydian saw her sweet face clearly, his heart filled with love as he bent down to his defeated foe and spoke softly "My fair lady has pleaded for your life and so you live, now go in peace" Medraut arose, not understanding his release, unable to speak, he stood looking at Rhydian, seeking an answer, but for him there was none.

Holding his lady close Rhydian sought comfort from her presence, bringing peace to his fraught thoughts, her love calming his disordered mind until all anger left him, yet still he could not find in his heart forgiveness. "You held back my hand, I would know the reason why, he was unmanned and at my mercy" For a while Gwen gave no answer, then slowly she spoke, "It seemed as though you were no longer the man I loved, a different person lived inside your body, for one moment I had lost you, for if you killed that defeated knight you would become as they are, using

141

might to conquer. I wanted my perfect, gentle, lover to return to me."

Rhydian looked at her in wonder "Your wisdom is from another time. I felt all powerful, as if no-one could harm me, the world was mine to command. My arm wielded a great weapon, its life force beyond my control, until it was a part of me, and I responded. It is an evil thing, the scabbard too, for no man can resist them, they must be taken to a haven where they will be hidden for ever from sight"

Then he wrapped the scabbard and sword tight in its plain cloth, seeming no more than an old saddle roll. "I must know, for you have not told me, did Medraut touch you?" He could not look Gwen in the eyes, his colour mounted, he took a deep breath, waiting for her reply. Laughingly she answered, "Cadair would not let him near me and my little warrior pup bit him, he regretted taking me and Cadair long before you arrived. Come let us return to my brother, for his vigil will seem long alone, then at dawn we travel"

Part Six

Journey's End

Chapter Thirty Two – To Ynys Enlli

The morning dawned to a grey and dismal sky a fine misty veil of rain hung over the nearby trees. In the distance the grey sky merged into the angry sea where white tipped waves threw their cold water onto the shore, creating vast lakes where grassland lay. Echoes from the past rang in Rhydian's ears, fearfully he scanned the horizon. "We must keep to the higher land the sea is restless, Annwn's gates may yet open." The wind grew stronger as they took uncertain steps through unknown pathways to Ynys Enlli. Rain began to fall in heavy bursts, unable to see they followed the path westward to Aberdaron, to the pilgrims church of St Hywyn, a beacon on the sands for those who made the crossing over the sound. But today there was no sailing to the island of saints, the boats were beached on the deserted shore, as great waves reached the stone walls of the church, its foundations buried deep under the sand, defying the actions of the sea. To the wet and weary travellers it was a welcome sight. Rhydian sighed "I regret that my purse is light, I will seek the Abbot, I have the letter from Llywelyn, his hand may stretch this far."

Leaving his friends he entered the small church. Sitting on a stone chair, like an old bird on its perch, was a small figure, white hair forming a halo round his head. "Enter Sir Rhydian, I know who you are and why you are come, my friend here has told me of your travels he will attend to your companions" He beckoned to a dimly lit corner, where two bright eyes knowingly stared out, swiftly followed by the black sleek shape of Menw. With joy Rhydian began to speak "I have missed you, and began to wonder if old friends had deserted me. Yet I have been told that I need not worry, help will be there when I need it most. Now I crave your assistance for Gwen, she has need of food and shelter, the others too."

The old man spoke "You are honoured young man, for only a few men gain the trust of an Eiddlig Gor. Come sit here on the chair of peace, an honour you are fit to take. I have a message to pass, now heed me carefully" They sat in silence as the seer gathered his thoughts. "This storm will last for days, and then the seas will run too fast for fishermen to risk the sound. Now is the time for you to go, tomorrow morning before Prime you can be on a boat sailing across that sea where others will be waiting on Ynys Enlli. You must go alone, this journey is your destiny to decide without aid or hinder. You are free to turn back now, for none will stop you, take your Lady home, take your rewards and make her content. Or take the last step of your quest; its ending is in your hands though it may yet be wrested from you." With his head high and eyes steady Rhydian replied "Show me the boat for I am ready"

The sky was dark and grey, letting no sunlight through, the wind blew hard throwing the sea around, as though a mighty battle was taking place far beneath the waves that crashed over the rocky coast, forming caves where sea monsters lay hidden, guarding gateways to the otherworld. Rhydian joined the others, now with Menw "Gwen, you must leave ere the days course is run, there is a goodwife nearby who will give you and Alain shelter until my return, for tonight I live as a knight at vigil and prepare for whatever the morn shall bring me. I am to make myself ready before dawn so now we must say farewell. I have a gift, to bestow made with rare skill and I believe, love, from long ago."

He placed among her long dark hair the circlet of gold, so long forgotten in its secret place, hidden in the

147

cold mine shaft. Gwen untied a leather thong that lay around her neck taking from it the ring of Emrys. "I have found it has warmth, unlike normal stone, bringing me comfort. I give it back to you, my talisman in battles to be fought"

Later he was woken from fitful slumber and collecting his crwth and pack he quietly left the church, following Menw's flight, down a steep, narrow path to an inlet. Rhydian saw a man, face half covered by a cowl, yet strangely familiar. He spoke "Come aboard my young friend, you will be safe with me this time" He flung back his hood, to show Gwyhyr's keen, far seeing eyes. "Barrinthus, the ferryman sails this craft, not I, he is wise in the currents around the Island of Saints, he can ride the waters as no other. On dry land I will be your guide"

Barrinthus, holding the tiller in one hand, the sail stay in the other, signed to Gwyhyr pushing them away from the shore and straightway into the seething sea. Finding a path under the waves where none should be the ferryman sailed the boat safely across the sound speaking not a word. Approaching the isle he found a sheltered place to land, then his passengers safely ashore he turned back. Words that it seemed the wind bore, drifted past Rhydian, "God speed, God bless" so quiet he hardly heard them, so deep he would not forget.

Chapter Thirty Three –
An Immortal Temptation

In silent companionship the two friends walked towards the Isle's higher lands, through the orchards where the Abbey's sheep grazed amongst the apple trees, they followed the path that encircled the hill. The sun's light slowly touched grey clouds, dark and threatening above the brooding sea, bringing light to a rocky cove. In this weed covered shore they rested beside a stream, the clear fresh water running from it fed a shallow hollow in the stone. Kneeling down to take a drink from this refreshing pool, Rhydian saw the surface move, as if a tiny storm blew, a picture grew in which he saw a cliff rising from the sea, with ancient stone steps leading to a well. Here, sitting all alone, was a young maid watching as the ebbing tide revealed Fynnon Fair, whose cleansing powers had sustained many a pilgrimage. He drank deeply, her image etched on his mind, a talisman to protect and guide him as he faced the final part of his journey.

A voice recalled Rhydian to his task "I must leave you to return before Prime, the Augustinians are stern in their ways, I am their guest and so abide by their rules." Gwyhyr's face filled with pride, as he laid his hand upon the young man's shoulder. "You have a wisdom that spans across the ages, I trust you to take the right course, and may God be with you, carry his light high and you will find a safe route to follow. As the ebbing tide recedes from the shore a bridge will show, lying just beneath the waves. You must cross this in haste, for only a short time there is an egress in the rock, a portal to where, I do not know. Here you must enter, whilst the water is low, before the tide turns and the rising sea covers the entrance once more. The Abbey Brothers await me now; I will keep watch and pray for you."

Sitting on the rocks, waiting as the dawn drew nigh, Rhydian travelled back to those carefree days at home, when adventure was but a story to dream about, battles were as yet unfought and love lay waiting to be found. He thought of the sword that lay in his grasp, of the power that it could bring, of the glory that its wearer could find. He felt once more that heady moment when the victory was his, when life or death meant which way his blade had fallen.

Holding the sword by his side, he arose and walked toward the sea, through the grey light of day break he saw a figure, still and quiet, watching him as he made his way to the shore. Long black hair flowed down to her slender waist, framing a face of glowing beauty, from which two dark blue eyes smouldered with desire.

She raised her arms high and revealed a body, lithe and sinuous, swaying to unheard music. He was drawn unresisting to her, letting the rhythmic dance drown him in sensuous pleasure. She laughed softly, entwining him in her embrace, her witchcraft holding him in thralldom, she laid claim to his soul, his mind, and for her use alone, his heart she stole.

As the waves crashed onto the shore, the wind howled unheard, around their heads, then time itself was stilled. She laughed, soft, yet triumphant, laden with promises of pleasure to come, of unknown delights and wishes to be fulfiled, she raised her arms, and at her command the storm abated and an unearthly quiet covered the land.

Into this dreamlike world Rhydian followed, all resistance gone, moving further into her embrace, held in a trance from which he had neither the power, nor desire to break free, his blood ran hot with a lust that naught could slake. Her face held between his hands he gazed, wonderingly, into her eyes "By what name are you known, your beauty is not of mortals, yet I hold and touch you, your caresses stir my innermost being, leaving me bereft of all senses."

"Do you not know of me? Look deep inside your heart, have you not dreamed of me since childhood? My art has grown over the eons, my favours bestowed on few men, for only the bravest can match me. I am Nimue, I am Viviane, I am Modron, I am Ninniane, I am Le Faye."

The rising sun caught her with the golden beams of day bathing her in light until she became as one with the sky. Standing in her reflected glory his dreams began to fly into the realms of history, to where the knights of old rode out to fight demons from the dark side of the world. The being beside him began to move, away from the sea, away from the pathway under the waves, away from the journey's end. Rhydian followed, held by invisible cords that bound him as surely as a silken rope, going onwards to a new life that promised him power and immortality.

With each slow step he took he felt the blood run coldly in his veins, all warmth was draining from him, leaving nothing but coldness in its place. He tried to halt, fearing to go on but she was so strong, her hand seemed melded to his, as if she was becoming him, and he her. He felt a great dread and prayed for help, seeking from his heart its innermost treasures to sustain him. Far away he heard singing, lost in the air, seeking a way to reach him, his soul called back. He chose the certainty of pure love, and rejected the black future of power, he chose the path of humanity, spurning forever the promise of glory, of immortality, so breaking her icy hold and setting him free to pursue his chosen way.

Once more he was alone, with nothing remaining of the faye. The storm returned, the wind rising and the clouds shutting out the sun, the tide was flowing, the rising water covering the bridgeway. Rhydian ran across, just reaching the portal before it was hidden from site, entering a narrow tunnel that led into a wide, lofty cavern. He sank to the ground and wept like a child, until, exhausted, fell into a sound healing sleep. The storm calmed down, bringing surcease to the island and into Rhydian's sore heart came peace.

Chapter Thirty Four - The Final Choice

As Rhydian slept the sun travelled the sky until it rested high above the cave far below, seeking a way through, to defy the dark, and bring warmth into its cold world. Rays of light spilled down from the roof, through ferns that clung tight to crevasses, turning the subterranean world green, rocks glistened with a myriad of stars, a beauty unseen by mortal eyes for many long years. The rhythmic swell of the ocean's waves pounded along the shore creating music that roused Rhydian from his deep sleep.

He gazed in awe at the crystal cave around him, steep walls rose to the high vaulted ceiling, smooth as glass they offered no footholds to climb, no escape, no pass to travel through, the way back had closed, yet he felt no fear, peace filled his mind, here no demons dwelt. The rock face shimmered and as he watched became transparent, revealing another cavern, lit by a flame dancing over a cauldron of liquid, giving an ethereal glow, throwing into relief a raised altar.

On this dais lay an imperial figure, a golden crown around his head, a shield across his breast. Rhydian gazed on the dead King of legend, yet on his face the blush of life remained bright, as if sleeping through a long, long, night. Seated at his feet were two knights, leaning on their swords, they too seemed to be sleeping. At his head two fair maidens slept, their long hair spread out beside them like cloaks that covered their slim bodies. Rhydian dared not move, afraid one sound, one movement, would break the charm. He recalled tales from his childhood, the Isle of Avalon, the enchanted cave, the sleeping Knights awaiting a recall to arms, to raise the King, to bring Camelot once more to life.

He realised at last why he was here, for now he could recreate the past, place the sword in his hand, then give him the water of life from the Holy Grail, and so bring King Arthur to walk again amongst men. He could be a great man in this new order, a powerful knight, a fate that he had long desired. He would be creating the legends that would echo down the ages, fighting for truth and right against the evils that beset man, and all the lands would know the name of Sir Rhydian.

With his heart beating fast with anticipation, he entered the cavern, passing through the archway he faltered, his mind uncertain, as he questioned his own desires. He looked at the face of the sleeping King, with the fires of ambition still burning bright within him, he stood beside the greatest warrior of all time. His childhood had been filled with tales of knights and maidens, dragons and magic, in his dreams he had been one of the guardians of chivalry, riding out from Camelot's hall to defend the weak and fight for right. Now, childhood behind him, he felt within him a new understanding grow, of another way, where no sword dealt the fatal blow.

Taking Caledfwlch, he looked upon on its hard, cold beauty, he remembered once more the powerful hold it had taken of his senses, a hold that was broken by a hand so gentle and a soft voice, by a love that could stand alone and defeat the evil of hate. Sheathing the sword in its scabbard he placed it on the still chest of his Lord, with hands clasped together in prayer. Taking the cup of Emrys, the Holy Grail, he filled it with clear spring water, now he must not fail to complete his task. Holding the ancient stone cup fast it begin to glow with a blue, flickering flame that cast an icy light over Rhydian, a cleansing, healing, fire, like a mountain stream that washed away the mire.

Bathing his king's forehead with water, he prayed for peace to reign, for the weapons of war to be laid down unused and the hand of friendship to be taken in its place. A gust of wind blew through the cavern, dimming all the lights, throwing him to the ground, as he lay there, a veil of darkness fell over his mind. He slept a dreamless, timeless sleep, no fears to wake him, with no sounds to disturb him, until daybreak.

Rhydian awoke in the cavern, empty now save for his own possessions. The king slept there no more, nothing remained except for memories, or mayhap they were but dreams, woven by the faye to entrap him in her power, or was she an illusion, a dream?

In the dim light he saw a figure, an old man, watching him as he struggled to regain his senses, to gather his disordered thoughts. Filling the chalice with water Emrys offered the cup to Rhydian "Refresh your spirit and sit with me, you have many questions that it is fit to ask of me now." Rhydian stayed silent for moment holding the chalice, caressing it gently, "this ancient vessel, I need to know the truth, is it the Holy Grail? Do I hold in my hand that which men seek, yet failed to find?"

Emrys replied "That cup was given to me long ago, to keep in trust, to pass on the care to one who did not seek its power for their own glory, who would use it well with loving intent. For once it held the blood that fell from a man on a cross, whose life-force is eternal, taking men along the journey in answer to his call. But - is it the Holy Grail that mankind strives to find? No, for that all people have within them, yet are too blind to see it."

With Emrys' words, Rhydian understood "It must be given to all people, somewhere good can reach out and touch them, I will leave it here, on this Isle, a place of pilgrimage where the fear that lives inside our hearts can be washed away." Then he went to the spring and placed the grey stone chalice on a rocky ledge where the water flowed into it until it spilled out, running over stones before sinking deep into the sand below.

He looked to where a king had laid, the great hero from legend, had he been created by his own desired wish to become the perfect knight who had inspired his childhood? He searched for signs, the cauldron of fire, the knights and maidens, there were none to be found. "I had in my grasp the means to restore to life a myth. Before I began this journey I was sure of right and wrong, that the sword, justly used, could cleanse the world of evil. Yet I have been enthralled by the power of revenge, I have felt the desire to kill, taking away all feelings of mercy and justice. To fulfil my quest I was entrusted to unite Caledfwlch with its scabbard, then return them to their rightful place, this I vowed. Last night I broke my oath, for his hand I left empty, with the sword forever out of reach, a choice, taken freely, but closing for all eternity the hopes of a reborn king regaining his rightful place."

He ceased speaking, waiting for Emrys to reply. The older man's answer was swift, "The long rule of magic has passed over. I have wandered for many years unable to leave my mortal life; your wisdom sets me free. I believe there are troubled times ahead, it will be a long, hard road for man to travel, where the strong must lead until they find a way to live in peace." They sat together in silence, until feeling release within their heart, and then Rhydian spoke again.

"I beg you, before you depart, to guide me for a short while longer, I must start my return journey unsure of my welcome back home, for I have achieved nothing. I even lack a place with the Prince Llywelyn, having upset his son I am not welcome at the court. I regret nothing, but do not wish to re-enter my father's house empty handed." Emrys smiled, "Treasures come in different ways, look to the knowledge gained, consider friendships made, the pledge exchanged by you and your lady, be not feared, your speedy return, I know, is much anticipated"

Chapter Thirty Five - Farewell

Rhydian began to stir, a restlessness was upon him, a desire to move on, to leave this place whose dim light began to fade even more. "I need the sunlight again, to feel its warmth, here it is perpetual night, a place of peace and sanctuary, but not yet for me." Emrys held out his hand "We will return to the sea cave, and wait until the tide shows the bridge again. I crave your help, my powers, although they remain with me still, are failing fast, your strength will take me to my friends. But before we leave I must make this cavern and its precious content safe from harm."

Together they left the inner cave, and with his last charm, Myrddyn sealed its entrance. "You see now a very old man who cannot continue without your arm to hold" So youth led age to the sea, as the bridge appeared once more. Rhydian carried Emrys until they neared the abbey, here he paused, watching as two old men came in greeting, with them was another, so wizen in shape and small, like a child, yet with black eyes keen and knowing that told a different tale, of one wise of a time long ago, whose race was no more, living only in the stories told to while away a long evening.

Emrys embraced his boyhood friend "Menw, the end is nigh, our time draws to a close. Bedwyn, you defend the sword no more, for it now rests at peace, its power over men forever gone and Gwyhyr, you are no longer the seeker of our heir, he is here as you knew full well when first you met. Our time is over, and we but tell the story, at last we can now take our rest and leave this world. A new day is dawning; we can only bequeath our past, our hopes and dreams to ease the hard road ahead."

With his heart filling with sadness, tears flowed unashamed down Rhydian's face as he listened to these words, "You will live forever, through songs and stories, your time will be as a beacon to generations yet to come. The trust you place in me, I have given you my solemn oath that I will endeavour to fulfil it, but I do not know what it is you want from me. I cannot land the blow to set people free, for you know that I am not a great warrior, who can lead men to victory. There is none with a truer heart than mine, I will give my own life for what is right, and for those I love, but that is not enough to take the fight across the land."

The four old men smiled at the golden youth before them. Then Menw replied "I have spoken with gods and demons, my people lived at the dawning of men's time, I have seen the strong reign, and the bad bringing fear to their realm. Through the years men and women who by their words and deeds have shown true vision, have spoken to you through dreams, for in your body runs their blood. Your lineage, and that of your lady, is rich and blessed. The hope for the future lies with your children's children, teach them well, keep them pure in spirit and heart, for they will travel to all climes. When the oppressed need men of courage, in times of peril or paucity of spirit, your children will answer the call, bringing wisdom and peace, to be a leader"

As Menw finished speaking, a boat came into sight, Barrinthus once more at the helm. He called to them "We leave tonight before the tide runs high, first I return across the strait to reunite this knight with his lady, who has kept late hours at vigil by Fynnon Fair and now eagerly awaits his return" The friends bade farewell with heavy hearts, yet for Rhydian, a renewed feeling of excitement as he looked to a future filled with such good portent.

Watching from the bow of the boat Rhydian saw his friends fade into the distance, becoming lost in the mist that descended over the sea in the warmth of the rising sun. "Farewell my true guides and companions, you showed me a fire's light which few have seen, that of the inner spirit alive in all men. I will kindle it well in your honour and from every spark, however fragile, we can build a mighty flame to cleanse the world in which we live"

Barrinthus smiled at the ardent youth, "You must first forgive those who do not have your strength, be their prop in times of doubt. The bright, fearless Llacheu lived in these climes many eons ago, Menw wept at his graveside and shed tears of blood, he too had the gift of song, this he has passed down to you through the years to bring heartsease to others, use it well, it will calm anger in another man's soul. See - land ahead, I must return for a longer, final, voyage, for now five old men can rest in peace, the last to know of the portals to Annwn. You will not be downcast, your lady and a long life await you."

Rhydian stepping ashore, turned to bid farewell to an empty sea, the boat was no more. Gulls flew overhead, their loud cries echoing across the bay carrying one last thought on the wind, canu'n iach, good bye.

Part Seven

The
Return

Chapter Thirty Six - Re-united

Rhydian stood in thoughtful silence, as memories swirled around his mind, a feeling of great sadness overwhelmed him, a profound grief for lost friendship and guidance. As he looked yearningly towards Ynys Enlli he heard a voice, full of love, drifting lightly on the warm air, encircling him with promises yet to be fulfilled, bringing to him his future. Through eyes, wet with tears unshed he saw his Gwen running with all the joyous abandon of youth.

As he stood laughing, she flew into his arms. "Rhydian, forsooth I do love you so, but never will I let you go away from me again no matter where you go, I will go, for I am not content to remain behind, alone. Each day I sat by the holy well until the tide ebbed away, then, in the fresh spring water, I could see you. It seemed you were leaving me for a far stronger passion; a powerful force had you in their thrall. I called to you, prayed that your choice would bring you once more into my keeping, I could not bear the pain of losing you"

Gently Rhydian wiped away a tear from her face. "I heard you call, your love carried me through a moment of great danger, my very soul was in peril. I renew the vows I made, I stand before you with nothing, I spurned riches, power, and glory for an unknown future and returned without worldly treasures to lay before my lady, I am indeed a failed adventurer." Gwen smiled with pride "Have good heed of me, you bring me treasure beyond price, I know of no man who could offer me that which you do, nor any other woman on whom fortune has smiled so well."

Then, into the stillness came other sounds, a boy's call, pounding hooves, boisterous yelping of young pups, the full baying of a hound, heralding the arrival of Alain. "I see our private army approaching, we must wait a short while longer for precious time alone. In the morn we journey home, I ache to make you mine own"

Early next day Rhydian sought the old Abbot to bid farewell, entering the church he saw a group in silent prayer, a bell tolled, its single note echoing around the nave. The dim light showed a figure lying before the altar, clothed in white, hands crossed on his chest, his beads entwined through fingers bent with age. Rhydian turned away for he knew he would not receive his blessing that day, he whispered "Godspeed, and greet my friends with love, take my word that I will remember, for they dwell in my heart evermore"

He left the church behind him, looking east to the shore where his party awaited, his stride began to lengthen. They rode towards the rising sun, like careless children set free from their chores, talking, laughing they wended their way towards the distant mountains. They followed the road trodden by many pilgrims, with other travellers taking the same route, they passed the time telling stories and singing like troubadours in small villages. They crossed the headlands, they played in the sea, they rode along the golden sands sleeping under the stars, making friends along the way who gave them shelter from the rain, a dry place to stay.

They worked and sang for their rewards, through the town of Criccieth, where the foundations of the castle were drawn on a grassy hillock, there to take command of its estuary as the Glaslyn swept into the sea. They rode in company, they rode alone, following the pathways first trodden by St Cadfan, watching the sun rise and set on the Llŷn as each day took them further away from Ynys Enlli. They spurned the high path from Nant-y-mor, the sea enticing them, riding behind the walls of Bryn ap Llyr's castle until the broad Mawddach barred their way. The gentle sands left behind, they turned toward Dolgellau, where Ythel awaited them within the cloistered walls of Cymer.

Chapter Thirty Seven –
Cymer Abbey Revisited

With great skill and cunning Alain and Rhydian hunted for game, a gift to supplement the plain fare of the Abbey brothers, an offering in return for the refuge they sought. Fish wrapped in fern leaves, moistened with sea water thus keeping them fresh and sweet on the journey. A suckling boar pig lay in Bronn's pannier, its squeals caused Cadair to prance and snort. This much amused Rhydian, laughing at his proud, brave destrier, so afeared of such a tiny foe. "It would appear that even the strongest may have their weaker side, the full grown Twrch is a fearsome fighter, and many a horse will not easily pass by a Mochen. Look, the Abbey lies ahead, our friends will be preparing for prayers, I trust Ythel is still there and not yet returned to Ystrad Fflur, where we will travel also, for I desire to talk with Brother Thomas, I have a boon to ask of him. We will bide here until past noon before we enter and make known our presence."

They dozed in the sun of early autumn, a sense of well being made them content to sit at ease watching the river as it flowed down to the seas. A sudden noise startled them from their slumber and a man's shadow loomed over them, "My prayer has been answered, I have kept watch every day for your return. Teg here ran fast, leading the way to you" Smiling he signed to a young, brindle hound "My good friend has a keen nose, though she has found many a trail in the hills, she still has much to learn" He suddenly stopped talking, a look of great concern flashed across his face. He stretched his hand down to the pup close by him, lovingly he caressed a brown head, wordlessly he asked a question, almost unable to hear the answer.

"Your bitch is fair, like the fable you have called her after, but you put me to shame here I have two pups, well grown but with no name as yet!" Ythel smiled, all fears gone. "I thought you might wish to take Teg back with you, for years I was alone, now I have friends, a home, a purpose in my life, my soul is given to the lord, for his service. My heart to this constant companion who gives me love and asks nothing in return, truly I am blessed above other men"

With great telling of tales they entered the abbey, where a much respected brother waited. Ythel led the way through to the Abbey gardens to a tall silent figure, who, looking in Rhydian's eyes gestured the seat beside him. "Sit a while with me, we have much to talk about." A smile lit the young man's face, "First I must ask a boon, of you. It is my greatest wish that you will soon travel to my father's house, I crave your blessing on my wedding day, your wisdom is sustaining me still. During times of danger it gave me great strength"

The quiet brother replied with a smile "I will be honoured, marriage is a state of sacred union, not to be taken lightly, your lady is most fortunate, or methinks it is others who will envy you such a wife. Now we will talk, time is short I am needed yet at the infirmary, Ythel will escort your party to the lodging house" Thomas listened as the tale was told, he heard as the voice changed in the telling, to where inner battles were fought, and won, until he reached the answers he sought. The young boy he first met, troubled and unsure had grown into a man, courageous in mind, pure in spirit.

Thomas thought about the young woman who had shared his journey, of the bond that ran between them, older than time itself, forbidden to him, and a fleeting regret came unbidden, the wish to have known such love, to have sired a son to be proud of. At this thought he chided himself, he had given his life into God's service and to the care of the poor.

"Ythel waits, I promise you will be well fed tonight, although I doubt the mochen bach is on the spit, verily his snout will be in the trough, for the abbey farm has need of a new boar." They parted, Thomas to plead forgiveness for his tardiness in visiting the sick, Rhydian to rejoin his friends, to eat, make music and regale all with stories of the Prince's court. They left late the next day, giving much thought to the meeting lying ahead, in the town of Brefi, did Aldan know of their journey, could she see?

Alain seemed troubled as they rode from the Abbey "You are strangely silent, my squire, what ails thee?" The boy looked at Rhydian and his sister, so intent on each other as they rode along, seemingly content with their own company. With a deep sigh he answered "We have shared a fine adventure together, but what role will you assign to me in your future? Will there be a place for me?" Reaching across Bronn's broad back Rhydian gently rested his hand on Alain's shoulder "I cannot tell you how much your company means to me, I well recall the many times your quick wit and courage has saved me, can you doubt that my marriage will make you less to me? You will be my brother now, and I trust my friend also, that is my answer" With a shout of delight Alain urged Bronn forward, "I have thought of something that is quite absurd, Gwen, if you marry Sir Rhydian, you will be My Lady." This caused much laughter along the way to Brefi.

After a few days journey the town came into sight soon they reached Aldan's small house. No light was lit, no animals to be seen, the doorway was closed and barred. Gwen ran to the old byres, she called for her mother, but no voice answered. The stable lay empty, the hayrick bare, in the straw a sable coloured cat slept unworried by their presence. "Where is our Mam, I am fearful, for this absence is not her way." Gwen suddenly stood still, head bent in the breeze, listening intently, then she led the way to the river bank gazing into the water.

After a long silence, she spoke. "I can sense her, but not see her, she is well." Tears of relief flowed down her face. "I have need of her, she showed greatest love for my brother, but we grew closer after he died. She must know that her daughter has found true happiness and share in her joy." Alain stood by her and together, maid and boy, they sent their thoughts for the river to carry to Aldan along the water, there for her to see.

Chapter Thirty Eight - The Fletcher

That night they slept in the stable on sweet hay, the chill of the early autumn night held at bay by Aldan's cover and the warmth of the hounds as they jostled for a place. Soft, rustling, sounds broke the quiet, mice running across the stone flags, watching for the barn owl as it flew home to roost. As dawn broke a man silently entered the barn, disturbing no-one as he gently settled himself in a corner, waiting until their innocent dreams had run their course, much like a parent watching over his children.

The rising sun cast its light though the open door, chasing the last of the nights shadows away, painting a golden halo on the sleepers. Rhydian, first to be woken, lazily stretched his cramped limbs, unfocussed eyes resting on the stranger, unsure he puzzled to make sense of the shape, suddenly he leapt to his feet, grasping the hilt of his sword, kept close by.

The figure spoke gently, "Be at peace I am no danger, an older, and wiser man, I cease to look for combat, even when I'm sorely tried I seek to find another way." A bright eye belied the age, yet the truth of his words was found in the stillness and easy manner of the hounds. "I have word entrusted to me for the children of Aldan, yon fair maid's beauty would soften the hardest heart, and so was her mother in years gone by. I loved her too well, even the tears she shed for another did not lessen the power she held over me."

As the sun threw longer shafts of light into the stable the others began to stir. Gwen, giving a loud cry of delight ran to their visitor, "Yvain, do you bring me word from my mother?" Halting, her voice faltered waiting for his reply. Gently he brushed a tear from her cheek, then replied. "Have no fear she's been gone a sennight now, where I do not know, but she set off in good cheer with word that I was charged to keep guard here, to watch for you to return, my reward to see your sweet face again, and to meet the man with whom I must now compete for your affection" Laughingly, he kissed her hand, "Good knight, I have oft wished Gwen was mine, but not for a sweetheart, as a daughter, tis Aldan that has my heart.

When my brother left to follow his Prince I stayed to give her comfort, and ever since have been near, waiting for the sun to rise on the day when it is me, not him she sees. You are much blessed to have Gwen's love she is like her mother's twin, and will give herself to but one man." Rhydian laughed and then replied "But I am doubly favoured, for I also have gained her son's friendship, I fear I will never escape, they have a grip on my life that I cannot break, nor ever desire to. I would consider it an honour if you would travel with us on the final part of our journey, I will keep my rival with me, surely tis much safer that way" So in high humour the party left later in the day.

A happy party rode along the banks of the Teifi, meeting the old road by the Clywedogau valley. Once again Rhydian travelled the path of dreams, but no ghosts troubled him as they crossed streams and climbed the mountain tracks. Passing close by the mines he told tales of soldiers and holes in the ground, of treasures found, rescues made, they camped on high ground as the light began to fade. Gathered around the firelight their stories grew, leading into the land of magic and myth, new music flowed from Rhydian's crwth, until sleep overcame them all. In the moment before deep slumber claimed him, a mantle of love covered Yvain, removing the pain of years, he savoured the warmth in his heart and slept until morn.

Their journey continued taking the well-worn way to Llanymddyfri. Yvain looked at Cyfaill and her pups, "Rhydian, your hounds must be named, they are half-grown, it astounds me you have not yet done so." With a shamefaced grin came the reply "I take the blame, when small they were but the ci bach, no name was needed, later, they had an understanding, needing no telling of our minds, just knowing, Yvain, yours shall be the honour, choose well" "You put a heavy charge on me, your noble hound dog has the aura of kings, like his sire before him, the bitch, is gentle, but with fire inside her. Alain loves her like a sweetheart, so she will be Carys. There will be no upstart name for your little warrior, for he will bear his father's name, he has proved he is an heir worthy to be called Cabal" With the naming agreed they continued to the castle, rising from a small hillock above the river plain, under whose walls many a battle for gain had been fought.

As the end of his journey drew nigh, he reflected back to the carefree youth he had been just a few months past. He mourned for that lost boy, who too fast had grown into manhood. He had put aside the dreams of childhood, taken with pride another road, leading to discovery of true friendship and love, a gift given to but a few. Yet would that be enough? He was unsure of his welcome home, for he returned a poor knight, no riches to share, no place at court, and no tales to tell of great battles fought. He looked at the old road he had travelled, lonely hills he had crossed in untrammelled days of freedom. Just for one moment he stood poised for flight, to leave the binds of manhood behind. Scarcely had the thought arisen when it died away, his future was here, with Gwen, they would face life's uncertainties, and build a foundation together, happy and fulfilled.

The river cut a valley between steep hillsides thickly lined with trees, where game hides from view. The river meandered, dwindling in size until just a mountain stream. Finding themselves in an open place they made camp lighting a fire to rest by. A grey mist, damp in the night air, encircled them, like a blanket cold and sombre, while an unearthly quiet descended on the forest behind, no sounds reached them. Gwen shivered, the hounds drew near, pressing their warm bodies close to her, giving her courage. Yvain's arrows lay beside him, spilling out of their quiver.

Gwen picked one up, stroking the feather fletching, "I remember seeking for these with my mother, but for her, only geese would do, but they chased me and though I was frightened I would never show it." At this Yvain smiled, "When we were children Aldan could cozen the perfect feathers from the hardest man, I could find the straightest Ash tree, knowing which branches to cut, then Bron, climbing higher than any other, brought down the best to take home. Bron may have been the finest archer for many a mile, but 'twas me who made the truest arrows. Many is the time we played Tourneys, with Aldan bestowing the victor's prize, always to Bron, she was my brother's devoted slave and I was hers, I never ceased to love her and I have no wish to be released. I still live in the hope that one day she will see Yvain, no more a little brother, and give to me just a portion of her heart. So I keep watch over her and hers and wait, for I am a patient lover"

The morning broke with the sun chasing away the final threads of the autumnal mist, a day to savour, where the air was crisp and clean, a gentle time before winter arrived and keen winds brought the driving rain, and snow filled the mountain passes. "I cannot ply my skilled hand to make arrows without the wood I need, I would explore these forests. If you are agreed Alain will come to help me, we will not delay your journey for long, lest you wish this day to reach Castell Du, a hard ride but within your reach if you dally no further but begin now." Rhydian laughed, "I find I have a strange reluctance to return, I feel there is a change in me that will not take kindly to a mother's rule once more. You go with your brother's son, you will enjoy each other's company. I recall hearing tales of an ancient yew tree that grows deep in yon woodland's heart. The morrow is soon enough for us to depart"

The two young lovers rejoiced in their company, too few were the times they had alone, a free day, with none to care for, was a rare treat. They told of their hopes and dreams, of sweet memories they held dear, of sadness and joy, they shared silence and soft song, as every boy and girl who truly loved, have since time began. Their peace was shattered suddenly, as Yvain ran into their camp. "Come quickly, I fear for Alain, he is hurt, I need your help, I tried, but in vain, to stop him, hurry" This said, he ran back into the woods, not a backward glance as the two followed, until coming shortly to a small glade. There, as if sleeping, lay Alain, under the shade of a giant chestnut tree, the gentle Carys beside him.

Gwen halted, with a fear she could not hide, "Is he dead" she whispered. Rhydian knelt down, feeling the still body, touching his face. A frown crossed his brow "No, though he breathes but faintly, I can see no injury. Yvain, tell me, what happened" Yvain replied "Twas the sweet chestnuts, he said you loved them and tonight you should have the hot and roasted by the open fire. I told him the tree was old and the branches not strong, but he would not listen. Up he climbed to the highest

175

one and leant across, then with the mightiest crack the branch broke. He fell to the ground like a stone, there he lay, with not a sound to be heard, and scarcely a breath passing his lips. Although I have no understanding of these matters, I know he is in great need of skilful help."

His voice faltered, "I plead with you Rhydian, for in your knightly training you must have gained knowledge in dealing with such injuries – tell me he will not leave us." Rhydian looked at Yvain with deep understanding for his misery "I cannot give such assurance, believe me I would that I knew. I learnt from Brother Thomas how to set a bone and how to cover wounds, but he has no wounds, no broken bones that I can feel, no, the hurt is hidden inside his head, he must rest undisturbed tonight. Gwen, fetch my blanket for a bed, Yvain, make a shelter, cover it with bracken then pray that in the morn he will waken"

Chapter Thirty Nine - Gwen's Mission

All night long Rhydian kept vigil, wishing for the healing waters that were flowing over Emrys' cup in that cave so far away. The long night ended as the breaking day lifted the dark shadows from the forest. Gwen stirred, her sleepy gaze focussed on the slender form of Alain, she laid her hand gently onto his brow, afraid to touch the pallid skin. Rhydian held her close, the rising fear that dwelled in him kept hidden.

"I have the need for help, with just my instinct to heed I know not if I do right, we were told as squires to make such wounded hold on to speech, nor allow them to sleep, for they might not wake again or keep their wits. Brother Thomas believed otherwise, that a body, rested, healed best. You must ride in haste and seek my home, fetch my mother, I can speak well of her powers, for she is close kin to the healers of Myddfai, wherein lies her skill. Cadair will safely carry you, trust him and he will be your key to enter the castle gate, for all know he lets none ride him bar me. Follow this pass between the hillside, be bold as you reach Trecastell's stronghold, take a wide track, keeping well away and travel fast here, brook no delay until you are passed the castle, then go eastward, along the river, the way homeward, until there, standing by its banks, the castle."

He paused for breath, then continued, speaking clearly so she could feel his concern. "As you approach the bridge, be careful to keep out of the shadow and uncover your fair face, show you are no danger, then ask for the Lady Elaine, the guard will call her to you." As Gwen listened rebellion grew inside her "Rhydian, tis hard for me to leave you and my brother, cannot

177

Yvain go in my place?" With a firm voice Rhydian replied "It must be you who goes, for this race Cadair, the swiftest of horses is needed, and I must stay here, for I have tended wounded men ere this. Now, be gone see, Cyfaill is here too, you are not alone" It was with a heavy heart he watched as horse and hound flew with their precious burden, they knew the trust placed in them, they would not fail to care for his lady. He prayed for her swift return and safe passage to his home, with her quiet courage sustaining her along the lonely way until she was again by his side.

He returned to Alain where Carys lay on constant guard, Yvain spoke softly "You must rest, the boy sleeps deeply yet, I will rouse you should he wake" Before the dream world could take him into its hold it seemed music surrounded him, so pure its magic weaved around his soul, a potent power, that came from the ancient days when man was liken to a child, simple in his belief, not yet defiled by the greed of all men. He slept until he was shaken hard, startled he leapt to his feet "Come quickly, I need help, he awakes, and does not heed me, Rhydian, I know not what to do"

Alain cried out, his unseeing blue eyes stared in fear; sweat drenched his hair and body, his arms flailed in the air. Holding his hand tightly Rhydian stripped off the covers, he bathed him with cool spring water, "We must keep him from harm, rather he was still than this, his mind needs to remain untroubled. See, he heeds my voice, Yvain, fetch me my crwth I will play to him, I know its music has the power to sooth all manner of men."

As the sweet notes flowed from the bow Yvain looked on with sadness, "Long ago my grandsire gave that to Emrys, he bade him search hard for the man who played with his soul, it was his greatest sorrow that none of us was such a man. Now I can hear the beauty of Joseph's thorn weave its magic again, from the dawn through the night it will bring peace and comfort, giving its own release. I have a boon to ask, that you will sing to us, it will ease my heart, and bring closer to earth God's healing power"

As Rhydian sang, silence fell like a cover over the land as every living being ceased for one minute, listening to a timeless prayer. As the sound died, there followed a profound moment, as if mankind was reborn all evil vanquished in a new morn.

Gwen let Cadair be in command of their journey, his fast pace took them swiftly through the green meadows that lined the river, heading toward unseen tracks following the ancient path thro' the narrow pass. He slackened his speed as the way grew bare; with the grass giving way to stones as they climbed higher, here the chill wind from the east blew straight over the high hill. Gwen shivered with the cold, drawing her cloak tightly around her slim body, until as the sun broke through the grey mist warmed her with its pale rays. The path descended to the river, to a trail that led to the long abandoned castle, standing guard over the river plain, having seen fighting over long years, now it was providing shelter for many.

Approaching warily, Rhydian's warning in mind, Gwen bending low over Cadair's side urged him on, he, needing no such spur, replied; travelling so fast that none could keep pace. Beyond the range of arrows, a headlong chase beneath the hills and woods, through marsh lands, until they reached the river, where the harsh track gave way to lush meadows where cattle grazed. The land was familiar, the air seemed to echo to words, "Hurry, God's speed my child" all along the water's edges the reeds swayed and sang, water, thrown by galloping hooves, surrounded her like a spray of loving hands, holding her safe as tiredness overcame her.

Desperately she clung to the thick mane Cadair, sensing her strength waning, quickened, eager to bring his charge safely home, a bend in the river brought the castle walls into view. A great Bailey surrounded the castle, a new tower arose from the motte, and a stone gateway sat between earthen banks. Over the deep ditch lay a wooden bridge, ready to be withdrawn if any attack threatened, with guards keeping watch, ready to warn of strangers approaching.

As they drew near a cry went out – "they come" – with the pathway cleared they entered. The great horse, sides heaving, shuddered to a halt, beside a woman, who waiting eagerly, took his rider into her arms. "Be still" she said softly "We are ready, come and tell all, but wait until you are within, the Lady Elaine is also keen to hear". Squires appeared to care for Cadair and Cyfaill. Gwen, looking into Aldan's face, too tired to question, sank into her embrace.

Chapter Forty - The Lady Elaine

With an air of command, as if sure of her worth, the
Lady Elaine came towards them across the bailey yard
until she reached Aldan's side. She looked hard at the
young girl who stood there, tall and proud yet bearing
herself with a quiet dignity, and found herself warming
to her son's lady. "Your mother has been waiting
eagerly for news of your brother for she knew yester
eve all was not well, but could not see him, nor you,
until you passed Trescastell fort. Then you came into
her sight, and I too saw and followed you as you
travelled along the river to Castell Du. When all is told
I will leave with my sergeant at arms, we can travel fast
and he will be my protection on the way."

Gwen cast a stricken look at her mother's face as
Aldan cried out in protest, "He is my son, it is my place
to be beside him" Elaine held her gently, "My sister,
trust me, I have much knowledge in these matters, I can
see to his hidden wounds, for there the danger lies.
Time is of the essence, there must be no delays. You
must prepare a litter to convey him home then follow
after, this will travel slower, and it will be some time
tomorrow before you arrive. Gwen will show you and
your company the way, be still this is how it must be."
Aldan replied, with grief in her voice, "Our friendship
has had but a short time for my belief in you to be
strong enough for me to give my son into your care.
Yet I find that it is so, I beg of you, ensure that he lives
for I have lost one son, I cannot bear to lose another"

Gwen watched in awe as Aldan, her strong mother,
let another go in her place, conceding to a skill greater
than her own. "My Gwen, we must fulfil our part of the
bargain, fetch warm soft bedding, we will get ready to

181

follow as soon as able, bring my bags too, for I also have many herbs and lotions, given me by Emrys, old magic is in these potions" Cyfaill, tired, but sure, lead Elaine's party, retracing the way she had but shortly come, as Gwen placed her hand on her mother's arm, "Alain is strong he will be causing mischief, I warrant, ere long"

Back in the makeshift shelter Alain slept uneasily, he stirred whenever the music ceased. The tired crwth player drifting into slumber only to be recalled as fretful movements returned, these were only calmed by the playing and the sweet sound of a voice, softly singing, so profound that they brought with them a healing peace as the hours slipped by, seeming to have no end.

Into Rhydian's half hearing ear came a hound's baying close by, with fear he listened, this fear turned to great joy as Cyfaill burst into the glade, and the boy within him cried as he saw the well loved figure of Elaine following. He embraced her, his words tumbling out one by one as he led her to Alain. "Hush, my son, you have done well, how did you know to keep him quiet? I have seen a blow such as this fell a grown man, wrongly cared for the brain will not mend, the mind is a strange and unknown power."

Rhydian replied, "I just did what Brother Thomas would have me do, the body heals itself he said, we just help it, until it feels right to leave. To stop his restless fever I played to him, and sang, as I remember you did to me when I was a child, it seemed to sooth him, I am very tired for if I stopped he became fretful again"

With a growing regard for her son, Elaine laid her hands on her new ward. "I can tell the blood of Nelferch runs strongly in your body, you have done well, now I see you are in need of rest, sleep well, I will care for Alain now. You must be ready for the fair Gwen to return. You could not have been wiser in your choice; she is all I wish for in a daughter"

Rhydian slept and in his dreams a young maiden placed a kiss on his lips, leaning over him with tenderness and great love, he smiled and reached out to hold her. The vision faded and he sought to find her again, he ran over the hills, calling her name, waiting for the chill wind to bring an answer. His name came back, soft at first, then louder, he sought for the caller, a thirst driving him onward. Then he heard a joyous laugh, "Rhyd, wake up lest we think Morpheus himself sleeps in our midst."

Still befuddled by sleep, he stared up at the image, puzzled, "Gwen, is it really you? Surely it cannot be, it has been too little a time", wonderingly he reached out to touch her. She grasped his hand and held it to her face, "I asked how long you had slept, it seems both day and night have gone, by my troth you are a sluggard, I arrived ere dawn broke, we travelled all night. This morn I found you here, senseless to my touch and snoring like a twrch, I have much to tell you, you must listen in silence to my story, for that is your penance for the tardiness with which you greet me" though the words were hard, a sweet smile belied them.

Rhydian asked her with concern "Alain, how does he?" A broad smile crossed her face as she replied "Fear not, his greatest danger now will be keeping two broody hens from smothering him, each sure they are the one knowing how best to restore him to full strength. Their rivalry in healing goes to any length, see here is one coming now" She pointed, smiling as Elaine, drawing near, seated herself close by. "I must return home now, Alain is over the crisis, and Aldan knows how to care for him. You two must also leave with me, Yvain agrees to stay, and I believe Aldan now sees in him a man to love and trust. He is rare, a man who can love without lust"

She was silent for a moment, then with sudden determination stood up, "Do as you are bidden, I will not allow the mother of my future grandchildren to stay one more night in these woods, my men are ready to return, we will be back by nightfall then we must prepare for the feastday. I recall my wedding, many people from miles around came, it took much planning, and I'll be bound this will be the same. You have but one day left of freedom and pleasuring, then you will be bereft of her company, for such closeness is not seemly, nor right, before you're joined in holy matrimony"

Part Eight

The
Wedding

Chapter Forty –
No Gainful Employ For Rhydian

In the castle stables Rhydian sat on the straw beside Cadair, Cyfaill's head, and Cabal's paw resting on his lap. He sighed and aimlessly kicked the dust away; mice ran harmlessly along the walls, seeking odd grains that fell from the trough. Rhydian stroke Cyfaill "My friends, can I re-tell you the story of when I first saw her smile? I have written a song to her, for all the while she is in my heart, shall I sing it to you again? But enough of this, I will go to seek friends, you remain quietly here, for the castle is full to bursting and yet more come, indeed it is as if the son of a king were marrying, not an insignificant knight, descended only from the princes of old, whose bride might be beautiful, but of birth lowly and unknown."

In the village he found the crowds had grown with all manner of visitors, minstrels, jugglers camping outside the bailey walls, mummers too, with garlands strewn across their tents, bringing colour and gaiety to all. With sights and sounds from far away, giving short respite from the drudgery and daily toil, every minute saved, to be retold on dark nights.

He walked unknown among the crowd, as people talked and laughed, they greeted old friends, and made new ones. Ahead lay the church, where children played outside, and within all was noise and bustle. No priest was at prayer, but candles and crystal lit the dark corners. All around were signs of festivities to come on the next day, bright nosegays and green foliage covered the altar table making all ready. Yet on the eve of his special day Rhydian was unnoticed, played no part, he returned to the castle with a sore heart.

There, drawn by the smell of new baked bread he entered the kitchen, where shadows danced on the white washed walls, thrown by the glow from a mighty fire, here batches of fresh dough warmed, until ready for baking. Taking a pie from the table, quickly, lest the watchful eye of the cook noted its absence, Rhydian looked around the crowded room, no hand dawdled. Then he spied a small boy standing by the fire, he, alone of all there, seemed sad. His attire was black with soot, tears streaked his face he swayed with tiredness, he tried to place himself beside the fire, but stumbling, fell to his knees in the hot embers. With a yell of warning Rhydian ran to him, and lifting him up, brushed the ash from his clothing.

"What do you here, so close to the heat? Your hands are sore with blisters, your feet too, firstly tell me your name" the boy looked up in fear as he replied, "I am Vonn, one of the spit-boys, I have worked all day without a break, with still more tonight to roast, and tomorrow the Ox, pray do not be angry with me." His sorry plight caused Rhydian much pain; that a child so young could suffer for him. He removed his jerkin, and flung it down, placing the boy on it to rest. "I will turn the spit tonight, you sleep. I have much to learn before tomorrow dawns"

Vonn watched in awe as the stranger took the lowliest of roles, a poor serf's place. Rhydian's soft voice began to sing, bringing a restful sleep to the child, others, all unknowing of whom the singer was, listened. Feeling a peace enter their spirits, they worked without cease. Later, with all ready for the morrow, they gathered in friendship, sharing tales and songs, lingering by the hearth. This was the scene that greeted the Lady Elaine, who seeking her son, entered unheard. The harsh words that rose inside her died before they reached her lips, for no anger could stay where love flowed. "Come my son, you have tarried long, your work here is done now you must return to the Castle, your Bride awaits you, so too the Priest"

Picking up the sleeping spit boy Rhydian answered his mother "Pray, do not chide me, for today I have learnt much and received more, also I have found hardship that I had not believed lay so near to me" then with Vonn held safe in his embrace, he followed the Lady Elaine to his destined place

Chapter Forty One - The Wedding Day

The sun had not yet risen when Rhydian awoke on his wedding morn, a mist hung like a cloak over the sleeping valley, the distant hills rising above, with the moon's silver light touching the peaks, as if covered in snow. He watched as the sun's rays grew stronger, turning the silver into a rosy hue, as the dawn broke on such a day that comes but rarely, keeping winter at bay.

Leaving his room he walked across to the silent stableyard, here, with his Cadair, there was no urgent need for action, no hustle, a moment to savour. All too soon the castle stirred and Rhydian returned to his more formal duties, the order of service, greeting the guests, yet still no sign of his Gwen, despite his requests to have word with her. She remained closeted with the womenfolk, kept apart, Alain laughed at his discomfiture, and vowed never to marry.

Noon approached, Rhydian donned his finery with pride and rode through the village, cheers rose from waiting crowds as he passed by, tears blurred his vision at the outpouring of goodwill that flowed over him. Turning to look up at the hill where the castle stood he could see the bridal party, led by the priest, wending its way towards him, flowers gaily strewn before Bronn, as she carried her sweet burden.

When they reached the church, Alain took Rhydian by the arm, leading him to his place, past people, known and unknown, their voices creating a babble of sound. Time stood still as he waited, longing for old friends, who were far away, belonging to another time. He felt, rather than heard his Bride approach, slowly he turned

191

his head in trepidation, he feared they would hide away the simple essence of his beloved's beauty.

He held his breath in awe as he beheld her. Her gown, glowing in the reflected light of candles, flowed like a waterfall. Hanging round her neck he saw a leather thong holding a stone ring, she wore no other adornment. Her long dark hair was worn loose, as maidenhood decreed, flowers borne in her hands, but in her hair none, just a circlet of gold, ancient, crafted in love. Their eyes met and they were alone, she placed her hand in Rhydian's and the wedding commenced.

With the final blessings of the marriage given, their vows taken, the pledges made, the first nuptial kiss lingering on their lips, ready for the wedding feast, a black feather slowly floated from high above. As it softly landed at their feet the candlelight flickered and time stood still. Figures appeared reaching out to Rhydian and his lady. A warm breeze caressed them, gently, lovingly, and the gates of Annwn opened. For a moment the two worlds shared a common realm, then the doorway closed, and time returned to their day. Holding the feather, Rhydian searched the clear skies outside in vain. Saddened he knew that Menw would fly no more, this had been the final goodbye.

They walked among the village people, speaking to all on the way, feeling humble in the presence of so many. They danced on the green, sang with the minstrels, they fled the mummers' japes until finally entering the hall, where their guests were waiting.

In the quiet aftermath of the day Rhydian and his new bride lay quietly on the great bed, now alone strangely shy, not touching each other, keeping their thoughts to themselves, feeling unlike the two friends who had shared dangers and laughter, who had pledged themselves to one another a short while ago. Rhydian turned with a rueful smile, "My lady, I am not at ease in this gloomy room, I feel as if many eyes watch me I long to show you my love, but here I cannot" Gwen smiled, her eyes clear and bright, she took his hand "Come, I know where we shall go, I too, long to leave this bed, we will sleep easy elsewhere, and I know the place to be."

Together, like naughty children bent on mischief, they dressed and crept through the Castle, past drink filled sleeping guards, to the stable yard, where they led a startled Cadair out through the gatehouse. They rode down to the river bank, the cares of the day forgotten as the moon lit the way to the place where Rhydian had first met Gwen, though she had been but a reflection of her spirit as she slept, so far away. "When I saw you then, I loved you, and as long as I draw breath will so do" There, where it had begun, united in body and spirit, they became as one.

Epilogue

The twin suns of Draconis cast double shadows from the space ship, throwing them long over the blue grass. Two young people stood on the hilltop, viewing their new homeland. They watched as the engines fired up, sending red hot jets of flame down onto the black stones of the landing site, unable to hear each other speak above the noise. Holding hands they watched as the ship took off, speeding into the sky, not to return again for many months.

The youth reached into his pack, and opened a leather pouch, handling it very carefully he drew out a thin circlet of gold, with a stone of the deepest blue set in an ancient clasp, which he gently placed on the girls long black hair. "In my family the eldest son is given this ancient symbol of love, for him to keep until he finds his soul mate. I want you, Ganieda, to accept this as the outward symbol of my love"

With a soft smile the girl replied "I too have a gift for you, in my family the eldest daughter is given this ancient symbol of love, for her to keep until she finds her soul mate. I want you, Maczen, to accept this as the outward symbol of my love" She took a stone ring from a leather thong worn around her neck and placed it on his finger.

Keeping each other close they walked through the strange landscape to begin a new chapter in a never ending story of their love.